# PASSIONFLOWER PETALS

# PASSIONFLOWER PETALS

JASMINE STARK

To my conflict avoidant self,
and to letting go of fear, doubt,
and rejection sensitivity.

# Contents

# Trigger Warnings

- Developmental deformity
- Themes of ableism and systemic racism
- Loss of a parent
- Panic attacks
- Traumatic head injury
- Near-death experience from a fall
- Ceremonial use of natural hallucinogenics

# Acknowledgement

Thank you to all those who took the time to read this book when it was just a work in progress. An extra-special thank you to...

Michele Stark and Ro Hotchkiss for developmental assistance and for helping me sew up the first draft plot holes.

Jen Maldonado and Jules Kleser for beta reading after my second set of revisions and for providing feedback that helped me give the story more depth.

K.F. Starfell for line editing services. I could not have asked for a better line editor, and I plan on using their services again soon. Not only did they help me keep my tone and prose consistent throughout the book, but they also helped me create a trigger warnings list and gave me tips on how to market my book.

Pam Jones, thank you for proofreading my book one last time before publication and helping me figure out where all the commas should go.

And lastly, my husband, Chase. Thank you for listening to me as I talked through my sticking points or brainstormed ideas.

I could not have done it without all of your support.

# Map

**1**

# The Invitation

"We've got mail," Aerin trills loudly, bursting through the front door of the Glade family house.

The sudden noise jolts Clara out of her early morning trance. The gears in Clara's mind, which are so rarely halted, spin back into action, and the sleepy fog that had engulfed her quickly disperses.

Clara sets her mug of tea down on the kitchen table in front of her. Glancing through the oval window leading out into the foyer, Clara catches a glimpse of her elven mother as she closes the front door with a large stack of envelopes clutched in her right hand. All but a strand of Aerin's short, sand-colored hair hangs loosely behind her pointed ears.

"Looks like there's a little something for each of us," Aerin says as she flips through the envelopes and slips her shoes off by the door. An excited grin spreads across her face, and she plucks one of the envelopes out of the stack.

Aerin glides through the foyer toward her nymph wife, whose attention is still firmly planted in her book. Aerin waves the letter in front of Iris's face as she passes her lounge chair.

Iris absentmindedly reaches for it with her free hand, but Aerin pulls it away playfully and sets it back on the stack as she continues walking to the kitchen.

Sighing, Iris rolls her eyes, but an amused smile sprouts on her lips. She sets her book upside down on the arm of her chair to keep her place and lifts her teacup from its spot, cradled in her lap. After a quick sip, Iris charms the cup and leaves it floating in the air beside her.

With a yawn, she removes the blanket from her lap and reluctantly stands up. She stretches her arms overhead, letting her large lavender wings unfurl like a blooming flower.

"Stella, come downstairs. You have mail," Aerin yells as she passes the staircase, entering the kitchen and bringing with her a blast of cold air from outside.

The sun hasn't been up long enough to return warmth to the dry air of the Celestian desert, but the earthen walls of their home still hold enough of yesterday's warmth to keep the cold from penetrating inside until now.

Clara's lavender wings wrap instinctively around her like a shawl to keep the breeze from her bare shoulders. Being only half-nymph, her wings are much smaller than her mother's and can't fully cocoon her. At least they provide some protection from the chill.

Clara takes another sip of her tea, letting the heat seep into her body and warm her from the inside. In just a few hours the heat of the day will make Clara miss this morning chill, but not yet.

"Good morning, Clara dear," Aerin says lovingly as she sets the pile of envelopes on the kitchen island and adjusts one of the spaghetti straps of her pretty, yellow sundress. Clara shivers at the sight of her mother's bare arms, but Aerin is obviously oblivious to the cold.

Elves like Aerin and Stella have a natural tolerance to both cold and heat, making the daily temperature fluctuations in Celeste easy for them. Clara often wished she had inherited this resistance from her elven genes, but alas, the only elven traits she seemed to acquire were her pointed ears and the inability to fly.

Aerin smiles and plucks another cream-colored envelope out of the stack, sliding it onto the table in front of Clara.

Clara's gaze falls to the envelope, and her forest green eyes glint with recognition as she sees her name written in a familiar script. The handwriting is unmistakably his, though, it has been almost a decade since she's seen it.

She lowers her mug to the table so gently that it makes no noise as it meets the counter. Clara stares at the letter but makes no move to reach for it. She barely registers the soft, fast footfalls of her sister running down the stairs.

At the bottom of the staircase, Stella swings herself around the banister, her long golden hair flowing behind her. She skips into the kitchen grinning broadly. As she comes to a stop next to her mother, her hair catches up to her and cascades around her shoulders.

"Good morning," Stella says with a smile, kissing their mother's cheek as Aerin hands her an identical envelope. It's the same size, shape, and cream color as the one still sitting untouched on the table in front of Clara. As Stella turns it in her hands, Clara can see it has the same handwriting.

Iris is the last to make it into the kitchen with her teacup floating along behind her. She makes her way around the kitchen island to stand next to her wife.

"Good morning, love," she says, wrapping an arm around Aerin's shoulder.

"Good morning," Aerin replies with a smile, handing Iris another cream envelope.

Clara's eyes dart to Stella as she hears the sound of ripping paper. She sits frozen as Stella pulls the letter from its wrapping. Clara's breath catches in her throat as her little sister's sapphire-blue eyes flick from side to side, quickly reading the words enclosed.

Stella squeals with delight. "Amor is hosting a pairing ceremony, and we're invited! That's so exciting!" she squeaks.

"Pass," Clara says with a delayed exhale, sliding her unopened letter off the edge of the table with a flick of her wrist. It falls with a satisfying thud into the trash bin below, and Clara lifts her mug smugly to her lips to take another sip.

"No, Clara, we are definitely going," Iris says quickly, rounding the kitchen island and reaching into the bin to retrieve Clara's letter. "I haven't seen Marigold in so long." Iris pauses as she recalls the last time they had visited Floria. "Twenty-eight years now? Has it really been *that* long?" She looks toward Aerin for confirmation.

"I'd say we're long overdue for a visit," Aerin confirms with a nod.

"Plus, a pairing ceremony is an important milestone in a nymph's life. We should all be there to support Amor," Iris adds, pointedly placing Clara's invitation back on the table.

As Iris steps away to refill her teacup, Stella steps forward and snatches up Clara's envelope. Tucking a strand of her golden hair behind one of her pointed ears, she begins tearing into the invitation.

"I'm surprised at you Clara," Aerin states, drawing Clara's attention momentarily away from the invitation in her sister's perfectly manicured hands. "You used to look forward to our Floria visits. I mean you basically learned to read calendars by counting down the days to our next trip."

"And the hours and the minutes," Stella retorts, pulling out the invitation and quickly scanning it. She must have found what she was looking for because a devilish smile spreads across her face.

"I know you and Amor have sort of lost touch lately, but you were a big part of each other's childhood, and I think you would regret not being there for him on such a big day," Iris says.

"Remember your pairing ceremony?" Aerin laughs, smiling at Iris and nudging her with the back of her hand.

"You mean our pairing ceremony." Iris chuckles, catching Aerin's hand in hers and spinning her around.

"Well, it certainly didn't start that way," Aerin jests, slipping her free arm under Iris's and pulling her into a tight embrace. She raises their clasped hands, leading her wife in a quick turn around the kitchen island. Iris smiles and rolls her hazel eyes.

"I don't know," Clara says "I'm pretty busy getting ready for the Beltane council meeting. As you know, I will finally be presenting my proposal for my garden design. Plus I can't leave the farming tower in the middle of the dry season," Clara says, grasping for excuses to stay home.

"Bullshit!" Stella interjects.

Aerin gasps and releases Iris, turning to reprimand her daughter, but Stella dismisses her reaction with a wave of her hand, keeping her electric eyes focused on Clara.

"I'm sure Jan and Greg can handle things just fine without you and if not, farming always has fae willing to fill in. And your proposal to the council isn't until the seventy-third of Laolisil. We should be back from Amor's pairing ceremony by the forty-third," Stella says, countering Clara's excuses expertly.

"Plus," she continues "I know for a fact you've had your presentation ready to go for years now. You're just obsessing over minute details, and what you really need is to get out of your head a bit." Stella moves around the kitchen island so she can put her hands on Clara's shoulders. "And what better way to do so than by being a candidate at a Florian pairing ceremony?"

"Candidate?" Clara's mind catches on the word, and the devilish grin returns to her sister's face.

"Oh yeah, Amor has invited us to attend as candidates," she says waving Clara's invitation in front of her. Clara takes the invitation and scans it.

Sure enough, it reads "Amor Aiday invites you, Clara Glade, to participate in his pairing ceremony as a candidate." followed by the dates and locations of the various events.

"Fuck," Clara whispers.

"Girls, language!" Aerin reprimands.

"Clara, sweetie," Iris interrupts, putting her hand on Aerin's shoulder to soothe her. "If you really don't want to go, you're old enough to stay here on your own, but..." she pauses, trying to find the right words. "I'm not sure what happened between you and Amor, but maybe this would give you two the opportunity to work things out." Seeing the skeptical look on Clara's face, Iris adds, "I'm not saying you have to explore a romantic relationship with him, but your mother and I would like to see you two repair your friendship, and who knows, maybe inviting you as a candidate is Amor's way of extending an olive branch."

Clara rolls her eyes. "Isn't the whole point of being a candidate in a pairing ceremony about exploring a romantic relationship with the host?" Clara asks.

"Not necessarily," Iris responds. "I mean yes, the point of a pairing ceremony is for a young nymph to find a romantic partner to bond with, but it's common for friends to be invited as candidates. In Florian culture, it's considered an honor to be a candidate, and some fae would consider it rude to invite an eligible guest as anything but."

Iris looks to Aerin for assistance, but their younger daughter tags herself in.

"Please, Clara, give it a chance," Stella begs, "Remember when we were young, and we would play dress up and pretend we were candidates in a pairing ceremony? All the dances and the frilly dresses. Forget Amor! It would be so much fun to actually participate in one together. Please?"

Clara hesitates, meeting her sister's pleading gaze.

It is a fact well-known and often exploited by Stella, that Clara has a hard time saying no to her younger sister.

"Fine," Clara agrees, bubbles of regret forming in her stomach the moment the words leave her mouth.

"Fabulous!" Stella exclaims. "Don't worry about packing. I'll handle the outfits so I can make sure our dresses complement each other without being too matchy." She kisses her sister on the cheek and disappears up the stairs before Clara can change her mind.

Clara glances back at her mothers, already regretting her decision while simultaneously worrying about what exactly her sister would be expecting her to wear. Her mothers give her sympathetic smiles.

Clara sighs, downing the rest of her tea in one big gulp before heading up to her room to change for work. At least she wouldn't have to agonize over what to pack, and ultimately, she knew her sister would pick things that would suit her.

Fashion was Stella's superpower.

Stepping into her room and closing the door behind her, Clara sighs again. She looks at the invitation still in her hand. Silver stars decorate the edge of the thick card, the dates of the various dances written in a beautiful bold font.

She sets the invitation down on her already cluttered nightstand next to a half-drunk cup of water and a myriad of scrap paper notes. She doesn't want to think about it right now. It's still thirty-some days away. Plenty of time to steep in her foreboding later.

Clara slides open her dresser drawer and grabs her work clothes. She changes, brushes her hair and teeth, and then she is off to the farming tower.

**2**

# Falling Leaves

The farming tower reaches high into the blue skies of the Celestian desert. Near its peak, sheets of waterproof fabric flutter in the wind, looking like the gills on the bottom of a mushroom cap. When it rains, the fabric opens up wide to catch and store the water for use in the hydroponics systems.

On a day like this, several moons into the dry season with not even a drop of humidity in the air, the rain collectors are nearly empty so the fabric lays close to the building. During the wet season, however, when they are full, the building takes on the shape of a giant mushroom with a broad mushroom cap, shading and protecting the surrounding buildings.

The farming tower is Clara's favorite building in the city and the second tallest after Daves Tower. Both buildings were built by her favorite Celestian architect Charles Daves.

Clara was introduced to his work during her first architectural design class and was drawn in by the nature-like elements of each of his designs. She quickly became obsessed with his work and ended up writing her final thesis on the human myths of the fae from which he draws his inspiration.

Her research told her that Charles Daves had spent his early hundreds in the Celeste Guard which sent him through the mists into the human realm quite often. During these trips, he was fascinated by the stories the humans told of the fae and also by their architectural techniques.

He said in an interview once, "Human ingenuity stems from their creativity and longing for making the magical real, as do their stories of the fae." It is now Clara's favorite quote.

Though he had not specifically mentioned the mushroom shape of the farming tower in any interviews, Clara theorized the design might have something to do with the human myth that fairies live in mushrooms or possibly the myth that circles of mushrooms are portals to the fae realm.

As Clara walks through the large doors at the base of the farming tower she wonders if she'll get the chance to ask him at the Celeste council meeting.

Just last year, Charles Daves made history when he was elected to the Celeste City Council as not only the youngest elf to ever be elected at only one hundred and ninety-eight but also the first hybrid fae. Until now, all of the council members have been full-blooded elves, but Daves was part human on his father's side.

The thought of meeting her idol made Clara's stomach turn. It was not just meeting him either but rather presenting her own designs to him. She desperately hoped he would like them. Her small wings flutter with nervous excitement at the thought.

Just seventy-five more days.

Clara enters the elevator, scans her badge, and presses the button for the twenty-eighth floor, waiting as the doors close.

A familiar melody plays through the speakers above her head, and she closes her eyes to try to place the melody. After a few more notes she remembers. Not the name nor the composer, but she remembers where she was when she heard it for the first time.

*It was in Floria. In the main house's ballroom where a small trio of stringed instruments played the tune, and pairs of nymphs spun and twirled around the dance floor. Candlelight danced off of the silver silk and mirrors decorating the walls as they turned round and round.*

*It was one of Floria's famous full moon dances. Their giggles sang through her mind as the two of them skipped and spun around the floor, hands clasped together. His arm wrapped around her, countering the force of their spinning that would otherwise push them apart.*

*A much younger Clara clung to his shoulder as they bounced and twirled their way around the marble and moonlight floor, occasionally bumping into the other dancers.*

*The other dancers didn't seem to mind, they would laugh and smile watching the two of them spin off in a different direction before continuing their dance. Clara and Amor were just kids being kids after all. Barely twenty years old.*

*Back then the only thing that physically set her apart from the other nymph children of Floria was the slight point to her ears.*

Clara smiles to herself but it feels like an empty gesture. The soft, joyful giggles in her head morph into a different type of laughter, the kind that bites and stings and rips your heart out of your chest. She shakes herself back to the present moment.

Her stomach lurches as the elevator decelerates, coming to a stop on her floor, and Clara pushes the memories back into the recesses of her mind where they belong.

The elevator doors slide open, and Clara is greeted with the soft pink glow of grow lights. The room is about twice the size of the

Florian ballroom, and instead of people, it's filled with rows and rows of white walls covered in green and purple foliage.

Each wall unit is about seven feet tall, three feet wide, and a foot thick. Tubing snakes through its center, delivering water directly to the roots of the plants that decorate its surfaces. Thin grow lights are secured along the sides and down the middle of each wall section, and they shine across the narrow walkways at the foliage on the wall opposite it.

Clara walks to her workstation trying to refocus her thoughts on the present moment.

Moving a few stray papers out of her way, Clara sets her water bottle down on her desk and smiles at the clippings of plants propagating in a wide variety of glass containers around the edge of her workstation.

"How are you guys doing this morning?" she asks, gently stroking a leaf of one of the plants.

"Good morning Clara, talking to your plants again, I see," Greg says from the table to her right. Clara jumps.

Due to the old elven man's short stature and the large pile of tubing on the desk between them, Clara hadn't seen him when she walked in.

"Good Morning Greg," Clara smiles, stepping back from her desk so she can see him properly. "What are you working on today?" she asks.

Greg flips through the planner on his desk scratching his chin with his free hand and ruffling his salt-and-pepper beard. The wrinkles on his forehead deepen as he squints to read the day's to-do list.

"Cleaning the old roots out of the irrigation system in section E and checking for leaks. Should have that section ready for you by tomorrow," he says in a gravelly voice. As he looks up from his planner, he smiles. His mist blue-gray eyes resting softly on her face.

"Oh perfect! Some of these cuttings are getting pretty big. It will be great to have a place to transfer them." Clara flips to today's page in her planner. "It looks like I'll be pruning the tomato plants and adding some fertilizer into section B. It should be a pretty light day so definitely let me know if you need a second pair of hands with section E."

"I'm sure I can handle it, but I'll let you know if I have any troubles." Greg smiles at Clara before slipping his planner into his back pocket. "Keep up the good work boys," he says to the cuttings with a wink before grabbing his tools and turning to head to section E.

"Oh, wait, while I've got you," Clara catches him, and he turns to look at her inquisitively. "I've got this thing out of town from the thirty-fourth to the forty-third of the coming moon. Do you think you and Jan can handle things or should I send in a help call?"

Greg sets down his toolbox and grabs his planner from his back pocket. He flips through a few pages. "You'll have to ask Jan, but my workload's pretty light that quarter. I should be able to pick up the slack," Greg states.

"Thanks, Greg," Clara says.

"Something fun I hope?" Greg questions as he returns his planner to his back pocket and picks up his toolbox.

"An old friend is hosting a pairing ceremony," Clara replies, fiddling with the pages of her planner.

"Oh, Super fun! It's been a long time since I've been to a wedding," Greg says.

"Wedding?" Clara asks.

"Yeah, it's the word humans use for similar ceremonies," he says and Clara can guess what his next nine words will be. "Back when

I worked undercover for the Celeste Guard, I went to tons of weddings." Greg raises an eyebrow "Ya know, a wedding is a great place to find a lover." He winks at her with a playful smile. "Make sure to have a good time," he adds before turning and continuing on his way.

"Thanks Greg, I'll try to have fun," Clara says with a chuckle, calling after him.

The chance of finding a "lover," as Greg put it, was slim. The only Florian her age who she got along with was Amor and *He* was not an option.

Clara grabs her pruning clippers and heads off to the tomatoes in section A. She finds the first tomato plant in the closest wall segment, and she begins to scan the plant for suckers. Almost immediately, she spots two sticking off the main stem and clips them, placing the larger of the two in her apron and dropping the smaller one to the ground.

Clara checks to make sure there are no signs of disease in any of the other leaves, and they all have access to the light shining on them from the wall section across from it. She then moves on to the next plant and repeats the process.

After the fifth or sixth plant, Clara starts to get into the groove and her mind begins to wander as she prunes. The discarded leaves float to the ground, and her mind floats to the past, to the last time she visited Floria.

*As the skyship descended close enough to the ground for Clara to see Amor and Marigold waiting to meet them, her little wings started to flutter. Whether it was from excitement or nervousness she couldn't tell.*

*It had been almost ten years since she had seen Amor, and even from this high up he looked so different. His pointed leaf-like wings were so much bigger, and he was much taller too, even taller than his mother.*

*Marigold looked the same. Slender, silver-haired, and beautiful. Her large blue wings moved slowly open and shut. The sight of her soothed Clara, and with a deep breath, she was able to slow her wings fluttering to a more steady rhythm.*

*The skyship continued to descend, and she could make out even more differences in Amor's features. His curly hair was longer, and his bangs hung down into his face. Branched horns grew from his head where two little stumps used to be. This was not the boy she pictured when she read his letters.*

*But it was him, she reminded herself. The same boy she had been writing letters to for the last nine years, ten moons, and sixty-two days. The same boy she spent her twenties and thirties climbing trees with. The same boy she built the fortress with. Her best friend.*

*She ran to the door, anxiously waiting for the skyship to touch down.*

*The second the skyship door opened, Clara jumped out, grabbed Amor's hand, and started pulling him toward the woods with a quick "Hello Marigold" tossed over her shoulder.*

*Amor was surprised at being pulled off his feet but quickly realized where Clara was headed and picked up the pace to keep up. He was fast enough on foot, folding his wings back to be more aerodynamic. As soon as she started climbing, though, he lagged behind.*

*"Clara, wait up!" Amor begged, ascending the rope net ladder after her. His wings were so big now he could have flown up, and Clara wondered why he didn't.*

*Maybe he didn't want Clara to feel less able given her wings stopped growing in her forties and would never be big and strong enough to lift her off the ground. It took her a while to accept that fact, but Amor had been there for her. He let her vent to him and cry on his shoulder, and he helped her see that even though she would never fly, she was still able to accomplish whatever she put her mind to.*

When Clara reached the top of the ladder she was greeted with a thick layer of leaves covering the rope net floor of their hideout. The clutter betrayed the fact that no one had been up there in quite some time. She peered her head over the entrance to see Amor only halfway up the ladder.

"Don't climb much anymore?" she inquired

"Not really," he replied, finally pulling himself up the rest of the way. "Been pretty busy with studying and flyball. And you know," he hesitated looking down at the leaves pooled around his feet. "It felt lonely up here without you." His bangs blocked his eyes as he looked back up at her, and he ran his hand through his floppy hair to clear his vision.

Clara smiled at that, looking back at him from the middle of the fortress floor. She couldn't help but notice how much older Amor looked. Not just taller, but more muscular too, and with his hair momentarily pulled back, she noticed his face was less round, his jawline more angular.

He looked almost handsome, and not everything had changed. His dark brown eyes were the same.

"Look at this mess! This simply won't do," Clara stated, kicking a pile of leaves off the edge of the netting where it scattered and fell to the ground.

"My apologies for not preparing it for your stay, my lady," Amor joked, grabbing a large handful of leaves and tossing them over the edge.

They had spent the next hour clearing the leaves and other debris from the fort while chatting and laughing with each other, only collapsing down onto the rope floor once their job was complete. It felt like old times.

"I've missed this place," Clara admitted.

"It missed you too," replied Amor.

"Oh, IT did, did it?" she questioned turning her head to look over at Amor.

*Amor looked back at her for a few silent moments before clearing his throat, sitting up, and saying, "We should probably get back. Dinner is probably about ready."*

*"Right," Clara said, sitting up. She watched as Amor stepped off the edge of the netting, spreading his wings and gilding softly to the ground.*

*"I'll meet you down there I guess," she mumbled to herself before sighing and getting to her feet.*

*She walked over to the ladder and made her way down to the ground. When her feet touched the forest floor she looked around and found herself alone. Amor had already gone.*

"Good afternoon, Clara" Jan's voice pulls Clara from her memories, and she turns to see the tall, curvy redheaded elf smiling at her from the entrance to section A.

"Good afternoon" Clara responds, wondering to herself if that much time has truly passed already.

"Greg told me about the 'wed-ding' you're going to?" Jan says emphasizing the syllables in the human word.

"Well, a pairing ceremony," Clara clarifies. "Did he also mention his time working undercover for the Celeste Guard?" she asks with a knowing smile, and Jan nods. They share a laugh before Jan asks.

"So this pairing ceremony, Anyone I'd know about?"

"Oh, yeah, um, Amor. The nymph I used to go visit in–" Clara starts, but Jan cuts her off.

"No way! The one you had a crush on!?" Jan shouts.

"I did not have a crush on him. We were just friends," Clara insists, but Jan returns a skeptical look.

"Isn't he kinda young to be having a pairing ceremony?" Jan asks, ignoring Clara's last statement. "I mean, he's the same age as you right?"

"Yeah, we were actually born the same fortnight, and you're not wrong. I mean it's not as uncommon for Florians to host pairing ceremonies when they are only one hundred as it is for elves, but most still wait until their mid-hundreds or early two hundreds," Clara responds. "Unless," she pauses as the thought hits her. "Unless they've already decided who they want to bond with."

"Do you think that one bitch will be there?" Jan asks, in a hushed tone.

"That's not very nice, Jan, you don't even know her. I mean I only really met her like once," Clara states.

"Yeah, but you knew immediately who I was talking about so you think she's a bitch too. Besides, I don't need to meet her. If you're a bitch to my friend then you're a bitch, end of story," Jan declares.

Clara laughs and rolls her eyes turning back to the tomato plants in front of her.

"I don't know if she'll be there. Probably," Clara answers as she snips off a large sucker from the plant in front of her and places it into the pocket of her apron, which is now quite full.

"I'm surprised you're going to go after what happened the last time you were there. I wouldn't want to be a guest at any of my exes' pairing ceremonies," Jan says, pulling clippers out of her apron and starting to examine the tomato plants further in front of where Clara was working.

"Again, Amor and I were just friends. He's not an ex. And it's been like twenty-some years since all that happened. I'm over it," Clara insists.

"Okay," Jan says skeptically "so you're going to go back to this place where your heart was broken to watch a bunch of girls compete for the hand of the guy who broke it? Sounds totally healthy," Jan says sarcastically.

"Well…" Clara pauses not knowing if she wants to tell Jan she would not simply be a guest but rather one of the girls "competing".

"No way!" Jan shouts, reading her friend's face like the front page of a magazine. "Did that dick invite you as a candidate? The audacity!"

"It's not like that," Clara interrupts, "My mom said in Florian culture it's normal to invite all eligible guests as candidates. He's probably just trying not to be rude. I mean my mom and his mom have been best friends since childhood, so, of course, he has to invite us, and he invited Stella as a candidate too. Plus, Stella's really excited, and I already told her I'd do it."

"Mhm," Jan responds skeptically. "I don't think it's a good idea, but it's your life. Just know I'll be here for you when you get back to help you work through all the inevitable trauma this trip will cause."

"Thanks," Clara responds flatly. "You gonna be able to handle the workload while I'm gone or should I put in a help call?" Clara asks, hoping to end the discussion on the topic.

"You're good. Greg and I got things till you get back," Jan answers.

"Great," Clara finishes pruning the last of the tomatoes and grabs the broom to sweep up the stray leaves and stems littering the floor, but Jan takes it out of her hands.

"I'll finish up here. It's almost three so go pour some fertilizer into Section B and head out or you'll miss your time slot at the rock wall. Something tells me you're going to need your self-care," Jan says.

Clara reaches for the broom and opens her mouth to argue, but Jan keeps a tight grip and gives her a look that tells her arguing would do no good. She has to admit, Jan is right. Some climbing would definitely help clear her head.

"Thank you, Jan," Clara says before turning to do as she is told.

# 3

# Arrival

Through one of the large side windows of the skyship Clara can see they are not the only ones arriving from another continent. Two very different-looking skyships float in the air beside them waiting for their turn to land.

One is almost pure white with golden geometric shapes decorating its soft edges. Another, a sleek matte black with hard pointed angles, dark crimson ropes connecting its balloon to its hull.

A third airship that seems to be completely made of metal with little to no decoration rises past as they descend, leaving its passengers behind on the ground below.

As Clara's skyship sinks toward the landing site, she directs her attention to the main house. She takes in the large stone structure and the beautiful murals covering every inch of its front-facing walls.

Her eyes scan the familiar paintings, and Clara recalls the epic stories that Iris and Marigold would tell them as children—the betrayals, the powerful love, stories of romance and liberation.

The murals seem to breathe life back into her memories. Like somewhere in the back of her mind, the stories are waking up, becoming real again.

The murals on the front of the building are old and weathered with some painted over a thousand years ago. They tell the history of Floria from when the nymphs first arrived on her shores to the liberation of Florian people from their elven enslavers. The ones lining the hallways inside are somewhat newer. Every decade or so, a new mural is picked by the council to be added to this living record.

It has been almost thirty years since Clara has walked those halls. Knowing there must be at least three new murals, Clara wonders what they might depict. What stories might they tell of the last few decades?

Clara can't help but feel her entire being settle and relax as the doors open, and fresh air enters the ship. Though she has dreaded her arrival in Floria since receiving her invitation, now that she's here, breathing in the fresh scents of Florian wildflowers, it feels like she has returned home.

A flash of blue catches her attention and Clara sees Marigold standing by the entrance in a floor-length sundress, her long silver hair neatly resting on her shoulders. Smiling, she greets her guests and directs them to their rooms.

Quickly scanning the front of the building, Clara finds that Amor is nowhere to be seen and lets out a small sigh of relief.

Iris and Stella have already left the skyship, pulling their bags behind them as they walk to the entrance of the main house. Aerin follows suit. Finally, Clara grabs her bag from the luggage net in the middle of the skyship and runs to catch up.

As they reach the doors they all receive big, tight hugs from Marigold. She smells like wild roses and apple blossoms, and her arms, though slender, feel warm and welcoming.

"I'm so sorry Amor is not here to greet you all," Marigold says as she releases Clara, placing her hands on her shoulders. "He is helping a few of the other guests get settled," she explains, motioning inside the building. "I reserved your usual suite. Would you like any help carrying your bags there?"

"Thanks for the offer, but I think we have everything" Aerin replies.

"We'll find you at the welcome dance so we can catch up," Iris says, squeezing her friend's shoulder before continuing through the main doors.

As they walk through the halls, Clara's eyes scan the walls taking in the details of the murals as she passes them. Remembering the stories that accompany them. They are all familiar, and Clara makes a note to herself to attempt to find the new ones once they are settled in.

When they reach their suite, Clara follows her mothers and sister into the main shared room.

Their suite consists of three bedrooms connected by a small but open shared space. The shared room includes a little kitchenette where one could prepare tea, a small seating area, a vanity table with an intricately embellished mirror, and a tall bay window with a splendid view of the hedge maze outside.

As her moms put their bags down and head toward the kitchenette, Clara goes straight to her room. She closes the door behind her, drops her bags on the floor, and flops onto the bed.

Her body sinks into the mattress, and Clara accepts the fact she has missed this place. As much as she dreads the inevitability of confronting the memories she has been trying to escape and conversations she has been trying to avoid, this place really does feel like a second home.

Even with the sense of ease the familiar room brings, Clara can't help but wonder if Jan was right. Maybe this trip was a bad idea.

She lets herself take a few moments before the existential dread fills her again, and she sits up. Clara turns her head to look at her bag sitting heavily on the floor.

With a heavy breath, she bends down to unzip it, pulling out the garment bags her sister packed for her. Clara walks over to the wardrobe that stands against the far wall. The wooden doors swing open easily, and she hangs the garment bags on the empty valet rod.

Clara flips through the dresses reading the labels pinned to them until she finds the words "welcome dance" written in Stella's spiraling handwriting.

Clara pulls the garment designated for tonight out of the bag and holds it up against her body, examining her reflection in the full-length mirror.

The dress is made of pale violet floral lace with a v-neckline, thin straps, and a ruffle wrapping around and hanging off the shoulders. The skirt reaches just above her knees and looks perfect for a summer cocktail party in a garden.

Dread bubbles in her stomach and she tosses the garment onto the bed. Clara looks at the time candle on the wall. It's still a good two hours till sunset when the welcome dance would begin.

Clara sighs, turning back to the dress. She can't bring herself to start getting ready quite yet, but what can she do in the meantime?

For a moment, she considers searching for the new murals, but that would mean wandering the halls of the main house where she could run into Amor as he guides the other guests to their rooms.

The time could be spent sitting in her room, letting herself spiral, or in the shared room, listening to her mothers speculate about the dance and the guests and the decor. She would rather throw herself off the roof.

Her eyes find the window out to the garden.

That'll do. Clara opens her bedroom door, stepping into the shared room.

"I'm going to go for a walk before the welcome dance," Clara announces. "Stella, would you like to join me?"

Stella looks up at her from the vanity table and shakes her head. "No thanks, I'm gonna start doing my hair,"

"Don't be too long," Aerin warns, looking over from the kitchenette. "It's only a few hours till the dance starts."

"I know, I'll be quick," Clara says, stepping out the door to the hall.

As soon as the latch clicks closed behind Clara, she sprints down the hall taking the route least likely to contain Amor. The hallway has very few guest rooms and bypasses the ballroom altogether. The colors of the murals bleed together as she passes them until finally, she reaches the doorway out into the garden.

Clara inhales the fresh scents of the flowers and mosses, and her shoulders drop into a more relaxed posture. Freedom.

Clara looks around to find the gardens are quite populated with other nymphs, most of whom she recognizes vaguely from past visits.

She didn't come out here to get caught in conversation with some older nymph complimenting her on how much she's grown or telling her stories about her mother. There would be plenty of that at the welcome dance later so she keeps on, running toward the center of town.

She makes it to the park before she runs out of breath and has to slow to a walk. Turning, she looks back at the main house. From here, it resembles a beehive with all the nymphs and other fae running or flying in and out.

Above the main house, the last of the skyships begins to disappear into the distance. Clara turns her back on the sight, wood chips crunching beneath her feet as she continues walking along the pathway winding its way through the park.

She occupies her mind by identifying changes that have occurred since she was last here. How much the few trees in the park have grown, the different flowers decorating the many flower beds, the new set of swings. It works well enough.

Without completely realizing where she is headed, Clara ends up at the top of the grassy decline leading to the ceremonial circle where rituals and ceremonies like the Passionflower Dance take place. It looks exactly the same as it did the last time she was here. She descends the light slope and steps onto the golden pavestones.

Her shoes click against their surface as she walks to the center of the circle and dips her fingers into the water of the central pool. A memory from long ago floods into her mind.

*"What are you doing?" Amor asked flatly, causing Clara to spin around, suddenly aware of his presence.*

*"Oh, hey Amor. I was just teaching Stella the Passionflower Dance," Clara answered, smiling up at him from the stone-paved circle in the center of the park. Amor wore a black suit that was slightly too big for him. His round face held an unamused expression as he stood at the top of the grassy incline surrounding the circle. His curly hair stuck up in several different directions.*

*"Why?" Amor asked.*

*"She wanted to learn for her pairing ceremony," Clara stated.*

*"The Passionflower Dance is part of the Florian pairing ceremony. You guys aren't Florian," Amor shot back.*

*"Well maybe we'll be candidates in a Florian pairing ceremony some-day," Stella said, spinning around wildly.*

*"Doubt it," Amor spat out.*

*"Oh, so you're not going to invite us as candidates for your pairing ceremony?" Clara asked playfully.*

*"I'm not gonna have one," Amor shouted almost before Clara had finished her sentence. "Pairing ceremonies are stupid, and anyone who wants to participate in one is an idiot."*

*At that, Amor turned and walked off leaving Clara and Stella alone.*

*"What's he talking about? Florian pairing ceremonies are so roman-tic," Stella said after a few moments, relatively unphased by Amor's declarations. "Wanna practice it again from the top?"*

*"No, I'm getting kinda tired. Let's just head back to the room," Clara said, grabbing her water bottle from the edge of the pool of water at the center of the circle.*

*"Fine, but can we come back and practice more later?" Stella begged, pouting slightly.*

*"Maybe," Clara replied.*

That is exactly the type of memory Clara has been trying to es-cape. She can't remember when it happened, but Stella was pretty young, maybe in her thirties or forties which would make it forty or fifty years ago.

Shaking off the unwanted memories, Clara turns away from the circle and starts trudging back up the grassy incline.

Back then Amor seemed so adamant he would never bond with anyone. So what is the point of this pairing ceremony? What changed his mind? Why is she even here? By the time she reaches the top she has decided: this trip was *definitely* a bad idea.

The sun is falling quicker than expected toward the horizon. Clara sighs. Her mothers would be wondering where she is.

"Too late now," she whispers to herself as she heads back to the main house.

# 4

# Welcome Dance

"Oww you're pulling my hair out Stella," Clara complains as her sister runs a brush through her tangled brown hair.

"Well, maybe I would be gentler if you had come back from your walk before sunset. The dance has already started," Stella says, restless with anticipation for the night of dancing and dresses.

Stella's hair is tied up in an intricate braid, and she has several tiny rose quartz gems laid out like freckles across her nose and cheekbones.

Her dress is also made of lace, but instead of violet, Stella's dress is a pretty pink. It is the same length and shape but lacks the ruffle around the neckline in favor of two short puffy sleeves.

"You two look so beautiful!" Aerin says as she steps out of her room in a moss green, ankle-length dress with a sheer lace shawl. Her short blonde hair is lightly curled, and she looks elegant as ever.

"Absolutely gorgeous," Iris adds, following behind her in a wrap-around summer dress with a light blue floral print. The green of the leaves in the design matches the green in Aerin's dress perfectly.

"Are you all ready to head down?" Iris asks as she finishes, pulling her hair up into an effortlessly perfect messy bun.

"Yes!" Stella responds, setting the brush down on the vanity and linking her arm with Clara's, pulling her out of the chair.

"Ready as I'll ever be," Clara says, reluctantly getting to her feet.

They step into the hallway two at a time with Aerin and Iris leading the way. Sounds of stringed instruments and friendly chatter fills the air as they parade down the corridor.

They step through the doors to the ballroom, passing several groups of fae huddled in various shapes.

Three sets of large double doors stand open along the furthest wall which reaches high up to the curved ceiling of the second floor. From across the room, Clara can see that several partygoers have already spilled out into the gardens beyond the doors, but the ballroom is still quite packed.

Some guests dance around the center of the room as musicians play popular love songs on a variety of stringed and wind instruments. Others stand in small groups around the perimeter of the dance floor, catching up and sharing pleasantries.

Looking around the large room, Clara concludes all two hundred and some residents of Floria must be in attendance, including another fifty or so guests from elsewhere.

Beautiful chandeliers hang from the ceiling, reflecting soft streams of light throughout the room. Purple and green decorations cover the walls.

To her right, a large staircase extends from the third floor to the second and curves down to the marble floor of the ballroom. A few elves descend from the second floor.

Looking up to her left she can see a couple of fairies hovering over the crowd lining the inside wall, their long, intricately veined, opalescent wings fluttering to keep them aloft. Clara continues forward to the center of the room, looking back over her shoulder to see what is drawing their attention. A family of dwarves stands on the second-floor balcony, conversing with the two fairies through the balusters of the railing.

Further along the balcony, she sees a selkie couple smiling down, watching the dancers below, soft white and gray furs wrapped around their shoulders. Near the far end, a young angelican girl sits on the railing, kicking her feet to the beat of the music. Her small feathered wings move slightly to keep her balanced.

Clara had not expected to see this many non-Florian guests, but this explains why there were so many different skyships arriving. The more she thought about it, the more sense it made. The Floria main house regularly hosts guests from around the realm, and Amor was always good at making new friends.

Clara wonders to herself how many other girls Amor might have befriended on their visits to Floria. How many of them may also be candidates in the pairing ceremony?

An unwelcome tightening sensation fills her throat, and she crosses her arms protectively over her chest. She's never really felt comfortable at large parties like this, at least not since she was a child.

As Clara observes the partygoers around her, she sees one of the older nymph women nudge a girl about her age and point across the room. Clara's eyes follow the woman's finger to the top of the stairs where she can now see two familiar faces.

Marigold and Amor have arrived. They begin descending the stairs from the top floor as the whole room looks on.

Amor is dressed in a well-fitted black suit with a lavender button-up underneath. His dark hair is slicked back rather than its usual curly mess, and his arm is interlaced with his mother's.

Marigold is a vision of beauty and grace. Her long velvet dress is the color of the night sky when the sun has ducked below the horizon but some of its light still remains. Her silver hair is tied up in a braided bun with tendrils curling down and framing her kind face.

As they descend the stairs, Amor's eyes scan the ballroom below, and Clara feels the sudden urge to flee. She looks quickly to her mothers and Stella who are a few strides away signing their names in a large guest book.

Turning in the opposite direction, Clara heads straight for the doors leading out of the ballroom and into the garden, hoping to disappear quickly and quietly.

Right as she reaches the closest door she can hear Aerin say "Oh look, Amor and Marigold are here." Clara turns to peek back at them. "Where'd Clara go? She was right here a second ago," Aerin adds, looking at Stella who shrugs and reaches for the pen.

Clara ducks her head out of the doorway before her mother can spot her. Once outside she takes a breath.

She knows she won't be able to avoid Amor for the whole trip, but maybe she can steal at least a few more moments of sanity before she has to face him.

Now that Clara is outside in the cool evening air, there is really only one place she wants to be, and it calls to her soul. She turns away from the noise and the lights and the other fae and sprints toward the woods. It's a good thing her sister knew better than to put her in heels.

*"Clara! I HAVE to show you this book I found in the library a few weeks ago!" Amor said excitedly the second Clara had debarked the skyship. He grabbed her hand and pulled her into the main house, up the stairs, and all the way to his room.*

Once there he let go of her hand and ran over to his desk to retrieve a large soft-cover book with a colorful image on the front. He brought it over to the bed and motioned for Clara to join him.

The two sat cross-legged on the bed facing one another with the book between them as Amor flipped through the pages looking for one in particular.

"Ah ha," he said, flipping to a page with a black and white image on it and spinning the book around so Clara could see the image right way up. "It's called a sky net," he said.

Clara looked down at the pages to see an image of a tree. Ropes were wrapped around the trunk and several of the thick branches with other ropes weaving back and forth, connecting them and creating a netlike floor. In the image on the next page, there was a man standing on the netting looking off into the distance as if standing on a balcony.

Amor flipped to the next page which showed a close-up of the netting and a graphic of how the ropes were crisscrossed and tied together.

"Do you think we could make something like this in the woods?" he asked excitedly.

A broad smile spread across Clara's face, and she flipped through a few more pages of the book.

"Well now we're going to have to try, aren't we?" she responded. "Where do we get the rope?"

Amor laughed, jumping off the bed and dropping to his knees. He reached under his bed and pulled out from under it a small sled, piled high with a bunch of ropes made of various materials.

"I've been collecting them and saving them for your visit," he admitted.

"And what if I didn't think we could do it?" Clara questioned, an amused half smile on her lips.

"Ha," Amor laughs. "When have you ever backed down from a challenge?"

*The rest of the day was spent working on their skynet together, and as the sun set, they sat in their first successful hammock.*

*"I think we did pretty good," said Amor, leaning back on his hands and checking out their knots.*

*"It was a good practice. Tomorrow we'll tear it down and start for real," Clara replied, laying back and interlacing her fingers behind her head, splaying her elbows wide.*

*"Well of course, and what will this new project look like?" Amor inquired, turning on his side to face Clara.*

*"Well, it will be much bigger and much higher," Clara shared, unlacing her fingers and using her arms to motion and point. "We'll start with a rope net ladder up into that tree and then we'll create a skynet in its canopy. And maybe next time I'm here we can extend it over to that tree."*

*Amor chuckled.*

*"I like the way your brain works Clara," he said, laying on his back with his head close to hers so they could better plot out the floorplan of their fortress. "But why do we have to take this one down?" he asked.*

*"We are going to need all the rope we can get," Clara answered, and the two of them were swept up once more in a fit of laughter. A happy silence fell over them for a few perfect moments, and Clara glanced over at him.*

*"Hey, Amor?" Clara said.*

*"Yeah, Clara?" Amor responded, turning his head to meet her gaze.*

*"You're my best friend," Clara said quietly as if it was a secret.*

*"You're my best friend too," Amor replied, smiling and taking her hand.*

Clara lays down on the netting of the fortress and stares up at the canopies above her. Silver moonlight shines through the leaves, covering her in a dappled green light.

Clara breathes out a sigh that melts all of the stress and anxiety left in her body.

"Hello again, my old friends," Clara whispers to the trees. A breeze rattles the leaves above her, and she feels in her heart they have missed her too. A welcome chill surrounds her making the hair on her arms stand up and almost making her shiver.

Though Celeste is much more technologically advanced than Floria and has twenty-four-hour everything, it doesn't have this. In Celeste, there are no natural green spaces. No forests, no fields of wildflowers, not even a garden. The closest thing is the farming building but even that feels sterile and mechanical. Clara hopes to change that.

Ever since she reached one hundred years old, she has been petitioning everyone she knows, trying to get enough signatures to be able to present at one of the Celeste council meetings. Soon she's going to get that chance.

Clara lets the energy of the forest seep into her, filling her up. She thinks about the presentation she has prepared for the Celeste council meeting. Wondering how she could possibly convey this feeling to the board. She has studies and stats, but the true value of greenspaces like this needs to be felt.

She lays there for a while, her chest full of a quiet blissfulness and tries to put the wonderful feeling of peace and freedom filling her into words the council might understand.

"I thought you might be up here," Amor says, peeking his head up from the rope net ladder entrance. Clara sits up, looking over at him wordlessly as her attention snaps back to the present problem. "Your moms were looking for you," he adds, pulling himself the rest of the way up.

"I wanted to be somewhere quiet," Clara says shortly, the peaceful stillness in her body now replaced by an accelerated thumping in her chest.

"I hear you loud and clear," Amor says, walking over the ropes and fabric that make up their fortress's floor. He makes the motion of sealing his mouth shut while taking a seat across from Clara. They share the silence for a few minutes.

Amor leans back on his hands looking up at the canopy, and Clara steals a glance in his direction. Up close, Clara notices a bit of stubble along his now square jawline. He's even more muscular than he was the last time Clara had seen him, and his well-tailored suit highlights this beautifully.

The image of a younger Amor in a slightly too big suit flashes through her mind, and her chest fills with anger. The words leave her mouth without her usual restraint.

"What is this all about?" Clara asks. "Last I remember you thought pairing ceremonies were stupid."

Amor wrinkles his brow in confusion. "When did I say that?" he asks.

"I don't know, it was someday I was teaching Stella the Passion-flower dance," Clara answers, turning her head to avoid eye contact.

"Oh right. The day of my dad's funeral." He hesitates for a few moments, recalling the memory. "I'm sorry for taking my anger and sadness out on you guys. You didn't deserve that."

Clara had forgotten that particular part of the memory and instantly regrets bringing it up. She looks back at him, and their eyes meet for a moment before he looks up into the tree canopy again. He takes a deep breath, letting it out in a quick sigh.

"When my dad passed away, it was painful, and I was too young to know how to deal with all those emotions and then watching how it affected my mom..." he takes another deep breath shaking his head. "He was barely two hundred. So young, and they had just bonded a little over a century before. It was so sudden, and the pain I saw my mother go through," Amor's gaze unfocuses as if in his head he is seeing another moment in time.

Clara can see the deep sorrow in his expression, and she wonders how this could be the first time she's noticed it.

"I didn't realize..." she starts but stops herself feeling stupid. How could she not have recognized Amor's pain? Was she *that* oblivious back then? That caught up in her own life?

She tries to think back, to remember if she ever saw him cry durning his father's funeral or the following days. If she could remember any other times he had let on that he was hurting, but that outburst at the circle was really the only sign that came to mind. The rest of her visit he had seemed oddly normal, but even at fifty, Clara should have known better.

"It's all right," he says with a sad smile. "I tried pretty hard to hide how it all affected me." He shrugs. "I felt like my mom needed me to be strong for her, so I just pushed it all down." He's silent for a few moments, looking down at his lap, his eyes still unfocused. "At the funeral, as they buried him, I made a vow to myself that I wouldn't fall in love with anyone like my mom had. That I would never bond so I would never have to feel the loss I saw on her face every time I looked at her."

Silence lingers between them for a while. Vows and promises are something all fae children are warned not to make. Nearly every other bedtime story they were told as children warned them about making promises, for anyone who holds your promise, owns you until the promise is released or realized. A vow to oneself had to be different though.

"What changed?" Clara asks.

"In the last 50 years?" He smiles and meets her eyes. "Well, I have. I've changed a lot since then, but it seems like what you're really asking is why I changed my mind about never bonding, right?" Clara nods, and Amor looks back at the foliage above him.

"It was something my mom said. Last year, I asked her if she would have still bonded with my father if she had known how painful losing him would be. Her answer changed the way I saw everything." He pauses, letting out a slow breath before continuing.

"She said that losing her bonded partner was the most painful thing she had ever experienced. That the loss of their bond still aches in her chest. She said that some nights the ache is almost too much to bear and then she said yes, even so, she would bond with him again." That far-away look filled his eyes.

"She said if the healers were able to take the ache away, even now, she wouldn't let them, because the pain was immense, but it was a constant reminder of the love they shared, and because of that, it was more valuable to her, more cherished than anything she owned."

His eyes turn glassy, reflecting the soft moonlight shining through the leaves above. Amor brings his hand up to swipe at his far cheek, and though Clara can't see it, she knows it must have been a tear.

"I didn't understand at first, how pain could be cherished, but then I remembered a quote from one of my favorite authors," Amor continues. "One I had never really understood until that moment. It goes, 'Loss is a teacher, a close friend. She shows us who we are and connects us to those we love, whispering in our ears, reminding us to cherish each other. Loss is just another form of love, and I pity all who have not felt her touch.'"

He shifts again, resting his elbows on his knees and looking down at his hands. "It wasn't really until that night that I let myself truly feel the loss of my father, and with the feeling of loss came memories that I had locked away. Memories I never want to forget again."

Amor looks up, and his eyes meet hers. "Long story short, I used to be afraid to let myself have anything I might have to mourn losing. But I realized if even the pain of loss is something worth cherishing, what was I so afraid of?" His expression changes to something hard and determined. "I'm done letting fear keep me from being open to love," he finishes.

Something in Amor's eyes causes Clara's stomach to flip over and her skin to heat. She pulls her gaze away from his, clearing her throat to dispel the lingering silence.

"I see," she says, but some confusion still lingers on her brow, and Amor keeps his eyes on her, patiently waiting for her to speak. "Why now though?" she asks. "For a pairing ceremony, I mean."

"Well," Amor hesitates. "Why not now?"

"We're still so young," Clara starts sparing a glance at Amor. A flash of smile sparks on his lips, and Clara realizes what she may have just implied and quickly adds. "I just mean, that we, I mean, you are only a hundred years old. Isn't that kinda young to bond with someone?"

Amor's smile drops, and he looks deep in thought for a moment. "Well, my mother had her pairing ceremony at one hundred and bonded with my father the night after her passionflower dance. If she had waited, it wouldn't have made his life any longer. If the future isn't guaranteed and you find someone you love like that, why not take advantage of every moment you can?" Amor says, shrugging and looking off to his right.

"So you've found someone then?" Clara asks, and Amor's eyes dart to meet hers. "That you love?" she clarifies. Amor purses his lips together and nods. Clara's chest feels tight again "And she loves you?" she asks.

Amor huffs a laugh, and his eyes drop back to his hands. He shrugs.

"I guess that's what the pairing ceremony is for," he says, wringing his fingers.

The silence lingers between them, and Clara looks down at her own hands to find them clenched into fists. The tightness she felt in her chest has dropped to a low pit in her stomach. She feels restless like she just needs to be somewhere else.

"We should probably get you back to the party then," she says, standing and quickly walking over to the rope net ladder without another glance his way. Her breath feels short, and her heart is beating fast.

As she descends she tries to get a hold of herself. Why is she feeling this way? It's not like she hadn't suspected this. That he had fallen in love. That whoever he had fallen for was why he had thrown this pairing ceremony. Why did it matter? They were just friends. Not even friends. Ex friends. Why should she care?

When she reaches the ground she turns to find Amor already standing there, by the base of the tree, waiting for her. Why couldn't he have disappeared like last time?

"So what's new with you?" he asks as they start to walk back to the main house. "Any plans for university?"

Clara realizes there's no polite way to escape conversation until they reach the main house again and picks up the pace slightly before responding.

"Not really. Just focused on work," she says.

"Oh? What do you do?" Amor follows up, keeping pace next to her.

"Well I wanted to work with plants, and in Celeste that means food growth, so I got a job working in the farming tower, though, I'm presenting a project to the council when I get home about developing a garden near the center of town."

"That sounds interesting," Amor states.

"What about you?" Clara reciprocates, shifting the focus off of herself.

"I've lived here in Floria my whole life and haven't had the chance to travel, though, I've heard a lot about the other continents from the fae who have visited. I'd like to see them for myself." Clara nods, and silence hangs between them for a few strides. "Maybe I could visit you on the elven continent," Amor continues. "Would you give me a tour of Celeste?" Amor looks at Clara hopefully.

"Sure," she responds without much enthusiasm. "If I'm not too busy," she adds.

The two have now reached the courtyard, and Clara turns to Amor.

"I better go find my mothers and Stella, and I'm sure you'll want to go find, well, her," Clara states, awkwardly stepping away. "See you later." She spins on her heels and disappears into the crowd of people without waiting for a response. She fights the urge to look back, and though it's stronger than she expected, she manages to avoid caving to the impulse.

# 5

# Miss Lin's Boutique

"Clara, are you even here with me?" Stella snaps.

"Huh, What?" Clara replies, shaken from her thoughts of moonlight through leaves, cold breezes, and warm brown eyes.

The boutique is quiet and cozy. A fireplace crackles a few strides away, and a million or so dresses cover the walls and line the inside of the store.

"What do you think?" Stella repeats slowly, motioning to the fiftieth dress she has tried on this morning.

"You look great in everything Stella, but I don't get why we're here. Don't we already have enough dresses?" Clara complains.

Stella gives her an incredulous look.

"One can never have enough dresses," she replies, turning and marching back behind the dressing screen. She continues talking while she changes out of the fiftieth and into her fifty-first dress. "You know Miss Lin's Boutique is where I fell in love with fashion. It was one of her seamstresses that taught me how to sew. It would just feel wrong to go home without at least a few ideas."

The bell on the door to the boutique chimes, and Clara turns her head to see the fae entering.

"Oooo, I love how she pleated this braided sleeve," Stella says, stepping out from behind the dressing screen. "See how the fabric is layered to create this waterfall effect?"

"Mhm, looks great," Clara says automatically without turning to look. She recognizes the nymph walking up to Miss Lin's desk.

Stella clicks her tongue "You're no help," she pouts, throwing her hands in the air.

"Sorry Stella," Clara says, turning back to her sister. "My mind's just somewhere else this morning."

"Still at last night's dance?" Stella asks, raising her eyebrows. "I saw you and Amor walking back from the woods." She shoots Clara a suggestive smile before disappearing once more behind the dressing screen.

"No," Clara lies rolling her eyes. Her mind may be stuck on last night but not in the way her sister seems to think.

"Miss Nightshade, nice to see you," Miss Lin says from the front, and Clara risks another glance toward her desk.

"Nice to see you too Miss Lin. My mother said my dress was ready?" Says the tall blonde nymph, her scarlet red wings curled behind her.

"Oh yes, come come," Miss Lin says, motioning for the young nymph to follow her over to a large three-panel standing mirror. As she follows her icy blue eyes sweep the room, and Clara turns away, ducking her head down behind the back of her chair.

"I'm getting kinda hungry, what about you?" Clara says as Stella steps out in the fifty-second dress. "You have to have at least a few ideas by now," she adds, and Stella sighs.

"Fine, I'll come back later with Mom," she says, stepping back behind the screen to change back into her clothes. "Can you hang these back up where we got them?" Stella asks, tossing a pile of dresses over the screen.

Clara glances over to the three-panel mirror as Miss Lin hands the scarlet-winged nymph an equally red dress. Miss Lin points her to another dressing screen situated behind the mirrors, and the younger nymph heads in that direction.

"Anything for you," Clara says sarcastically, picking up the dresses. If she is quick about it, maybe she could get out of the store without having to interact with Miss Nightshade.

Clara starts hanging up the dresses in their designated spots, working her way through the boutique.

"Clara dear, did you and your sister find everything you were looking for?" Miss Lin asks.

"Yes ma'am," Clara says, quickly hanging up the last few dresses.

"You are an absolute genius, Miss Lin," Stella says, popping up beside Clara in her yellow romper. "I would love to pick your brain if you have some time this week."

"Oh you're always so sweet Stella, it is so great to see you again." Miss Lin says smiling with a slight blush on her cheeks. "You know I'm always happy to answer your questions. Will you two be at the Name Dance tomorrow?" she asks.

"Of course," Stella says, "Clara and I are both candidates."

Clara eyes the dressing screen behind Miss Lin.

"I'll be outside," she whispers to her sister, who waves her off.

"Have you been busy making dresses for the other candidates this moon?" Stella asks. "I saw at least a couple of dresses last night with your name written all over them."

"Oh yes," Miss Lin says as Clara rushes to the front of the boutique. The bell above Clara's head chimes as she pulls the glass door open and Miss Lin says "I've even had some custom requests for candidate dresses like this one. Gosh, Vira, you look gorgeous."

Vira, so that was her name. Clara didn't need to look to know Miss Lin spoke the truth. When she first saw the nymph almost thirty years ago she thought she was perfectly pretty. However, when she saw her dancing with Amor at the welcome dance last night, she looked nauseatingly beautiful.

When Jan asked if she would be attending the pairing ceremony, Clara figured the nymph was going to be a candidate, but having her assumption confirmed stings more than she expected. Something twists deep in her stomach, and she quickly steps out the door not caring when it slams closed behind her.

Clara opens her notebook, starting to sketch the same thing she's been sketching for about a decade. Stella slides into the chair across from her at the small eatery.

"So that's where your head's been?" Stella asks.

"Huh?" Clara says looking up. Stella laughs and shakes her head.

"Back at Miss Lin's, you said your mind was elsewhere and that it wasn't at last night's dance. Was it in your garden?"

"Oh, yeah," Clara replies, setting her pencil down. "Sorry, I just really want my proposal to be accepted."

"I know," Stella says with a soft smile. "You've wanted this for a long time now."

"Yeah, and now that I'm finally one hundred, maybe the council will take me seriously," Clara says, wringing her fingers.

"I'm sure if anyone can convince them, It's you," Stella says, reaching across the table and grabbing Clara's hand. "And even if they don't accept the proposal this time, I've never known you to be the type to give up on what you want."

Clara nods and smiles at her sister.

"You're right," she says. "Celeste is getting a garden if it's the last thing I do."

"I have no doubt," Stella replies, her smile growing as she sits back in her chair.

Clara sits up a little taller and closes her notebook.

"So how have things been going at the clothing house?" she asks and Stella slouches forward slightly.

"It's alright. I mean I just started working there so I can't expect to be given my preferred job right away, you know?" Stella says. "Gotta pay my dues first."

"So what sort of jobs do they have you doing?" Clara asks as she slips her notebook back into her bag.

"Primarily sorting and repairs," Stella says.

A young nymph steps up to their table and slides their plates in front of them.

"Thank you," the sisters say in unison.

"You're very welcome, enjoy your food." The young nymph smiles before returning to the kitchen.

Stella turns back to Clara, grabbing her spoon and dipping into her soup. "It gets repetitive and boring sometimes, but I won't be doing it forever, I'm sure you had similar mundane tasks when you first started at the farming tower," she says.

Clara nods as she takes a bite of her sandwich.

"Yeah, they had me sweeping floors and cleaning out old roots for a while. I'm sure you'll get some more interesting tasks soon," Clara says before taking another bite.

"I know, ultimately I wanna be on the design team, but I have a feeling I'll have to wait several decades for that. The youngest fae on the design team currently is one hundred and thirty so it could be a while," Stella says, slouching forward more.

"I'm sure it won't be that long Stell," Clara says with a smile, "As soon as they see what you can do, they'll be begging you to be on the team."

"Thanks, sis," Stella says, sitting a little taller. "You know, I designed a couple of dresses for the pairing ceremony. I think they turned out pretty well."

"Really?" Clara says, setting down her sandwich. "Where did you get the fabric?" she asks.

Stella smiles.

"Well technically mine was an assignment for my dress design class, but I asked Mrs. Hellen if I could make a second dress for you," Stella said with a smile. "I told her about the pairing ceremony, and she insisted I make you a dress as well as long as I let her present them to the class."

"That's awesome Stell," Clara says. "I'm excited to see it. Which dance is it for?" Clara asks, taking the last bite of her sandwich.

"Mileway Dance," Stella replies, also finishing her soup.

"Saving the best for last I see," Clara says with a smile.

# 6

## Name Dance

Clara examines herself in the standing mirror, uncomfortable with the way this dress clings tightly to her body.

The dress is a deep plum color and the same length as the one she wore last night except it's made out of a solid stretchy fabric. A pair of built-in shorts, that are somewhat snug, are fitted beneath the flowy, mildly translucent skirt.

It looks like something a dancer may wear during a performance.

Fitting, tonight would be a performance. But why did it have to be so clingy and figure-hugging?

Tonight would be the Name Dance. This would be the first event with a "winner", though Clara was certain she did not want the prize.

The "winners" of tonight's Name Dance and the following night's Trivia Dance would be awarded honorary spots in the Passionflower Dance. It was a prize that sounded more like a punishment to Clara.

She shudders at the thought of performing the Passionflower Dance in front of Amor and the rest of the guests. It makes her face feel hot, and she swallows hard. She wonders when the last time was, that she felt comfortable dancing in public.

Shaking her head to clear her mind of the thought, she tries to refocus her attention on tonight's nightmare, which could be embarrassing enough.

The name dance would begin with Amor and the pairing ceremony candidates introducing themselves to each other using a form of dance language that had been developed in Floria over the centuries.

Though they had not grown up in Floria, Clara and her sister had learned some of the dance signs at the full moon dances they had attended during their visits.

On one visit when they were in their early twenties, Amor taught her about the Name Dance tradition and helped her create a name dance of her own.

*As Clara and Amor walked through the forest to their favorite climbing tree, Amor excitedly rambled about what he had learned in school since the last time Clara and her family had visited.*

*He was especially excited to teach Clara the hand signs he had learned in class.*

*"They're part of the Florian dance language and each one represents a letter or a sound," Amor said.*

*Clara couldn't help but smile and listen intently whenever Amor got like this. He had the same passion for learning as she did and was always eager to share what he had learned with her.*

*His face lit up when he started talking about the Name Dance tradition and how, after learning the hand signs, each of the students got to come up with their own name dance. The teachers helped them pick a few of their favorite dance signs and incorporated the hand signs spelling their names, combining them together.*

"So the hand signs for my name are A. M. O. and R," he said, signing the letters for Clara. Clara watched and copied the shapes he made with his hands. "Yeah, like that," he said, smiling as she copied the last letter.

"And I like climbing trees and reading so I was thinking I could do this." He reached up with his right hand and lifted his other leg while he made the A sign with both hands. He switched sides so his left arm was stretched towards the sky and lifted his right foot off the ground. As he did so, he also changed his hand signs to Ms,

"That's climbing," he explained, as if it wasn't completely obvious. "And then I could do this." He reached both hands up with the O hand sign spreading his arms in a Y over his head and spinning in a circle. "That's tree. And then, I could end with the sign for reading." He brings his hands together palms touching with his middle finger sitting on top of his pointer, the R hand sign. He parts his hands opening them like a book. "What do you think?" he asked Clara when he finished.

"It's perfect for you," Clara replied, smiling and repeating the dance.

Later, when they were back at the main house, Amor and Clara worked together to create a dance for Clara's name. Stella was only eight at the time, but she watched intently and copied the movements her sister made as best she could.


Clara wonders if Amor's name dance has changed much since he had taught it to her. They were so little back then and he had said himself that he has changed a lot over the last fifty years.

Clara starts to move slowly through the name dance Amor had taught her almost eighty years ago, watching herself in the mirror. When she finishes his name, she dances her own and it comes back to her mind only as her body moves through the motions. It surprises her, how her body remembers the dance on its own. She had practiced it many times in the privacy of her room but not for decades.

"You look so pretty!" Stella says from the doorway, startling Clara. She continues gliding into Clara's room. "How's it feel? I know this type of fabric can feel a bit snug when you first put it on," Stella asks.

Stella's dress is similar in style to Clara's with the same type of fabric, except hers is a vibrant shade of hot pink. It also has pieces of translucent fabric flowing from the skirt of her dress to cuffs around her wrists.

"It's alright," Clara says.

"Were you just practicing your name dance?" Stella asks. "I think I've got mine down, but I haven't decided whether to end it with the dance sign for bubbly." Stella does a quick spin waving her arms in front of her in a wave motion, her hands fisted in the sign for A "or the sign for fireworks." She drops down to touch the ground before popping up with one arm held in the air, her fingers splayed wide and her other hand held forward with the A sign.

"They both look great Stella," Clara says looking back to the mirror and pulling on the hem of her shorts to adjust them. Her sister was always very creative and expressed herself fearlessly and unapologetically. She has a self-assuredness and confidence Clara envies.

The thought of having to perform her name dance in front of so many fae makes Clara's stomach churn. She hasn't even thought about whether or not she should update hers, but it is too late now. Best to stick with what she knows.

At least she can be pretty sure she isn't going to be "winning" the spot in the Passionflower Dance with her old name dance.

The theme of tonight's decorations must be skyships. At least twenty models float through the air above the dance floor, occasionally bumping into each other and gliding in different directions. Blue and white drapes adorn the walls and balusters creating a skyline backdrop for the mini skyships.

Clara watches from the edge of the dancefloor as a young angelican girl reaches out from the balcony to touch a skyship that looks remarkably similar to the white and gold one she saw in the skies yesterday. With a swish of her wrist, it changes directions and collides with another miniature that looks like the one she and her family usually take to Floria. They rebound off each other moving, unharmed, in different directions.

"Hello Clara and Stella," Amor says, coming up behind them. When Clara turns to meet his eyes he smiles broadly at her. He must not have noticed she had been actively avoiding him after she ditched him last night. "Are you two looking forward to the Name Dance?" he asks.

"Absolutely" Stella exclaims "I've been honing my pattern since I got your invitation. I'm really looking forward to showing it off."

"I'm excited to see it." Amor laughs joyfully before looking over at Clara with a smile.

She opens her mouth but can't think of what to say. Luckily she doesn't have to as a voice calls out for the Name Dance to begin.

"I'd like to ask all guests to exit the dance floor and all candidates to create a large circle around me. And Amor..." Madame Rose says, from the center of the floor, looking around until her sharp brown eyes find the nymph she is looking for. "Amor, come stand in the middle of the circle with me."

Clara looks up at Amor whose attention is now directed at Madame Rose. He takes a deep breath, and for a second Clara can see her anxiety and nervousness reflected in his face.

The crack in Amor's confident demeanor only lasts a second, but it catches Clara off guard. She realizes Amor has more reason to be nervous than her.

She would only have everyone's eyes on her for the short time it would take for her to perform her name and copy his. He is literally going to be the center of attention for the entire Name Dance.

He looks back at her with a smile and says "See you out there," before turning and heading straight for the center of the dance floor.

Clara watches him as he joins Madame Rose until Stella loops her arm through hers and pulls her into place in the circle of candidates, forming around the edge of the dance floor.

Once in place, Clara glances around the circle. There are twelve other candidates not including herself and Stella. Clara only recognizes a few.

Vira, the nymph from Miss Lin's Boutique, is, of course, one. Next to her is another nymph girl Clara met during her last visit to Floria. She remembered her as shy. It seems that has not changed. The brunette nymph stands looking down at the floor as she waits for the music to start, her leafy wings folded downward and hanging behind her back.

Clara's eyes return to the thin blonde, remembering their short interaction after Amor's flyball game. She hadn't said anything to Clara, but when the girl's ice-blue eyes landed on her, Clara could almost feel the cold daggers hitting her skin.

Vira starts looking around the circle at the faces of the other candidates. She and Clara almost lock eyes, but Clara quickly looks away before the icey blue eyes land on her once more.

The other candidate's faces range from vaguely familiar to completely foreign. About half of the other candidates are nymphs, each with a set of petal or leaf-like wings ranging in color and shade. The others are a mix of other fae.

There are a couple of wingless fae in the mix, like Stella. One is a mer girl with green scales on her shoulders, elbows, and knees.

The other is a girl who looks almost like an elf except her eyes are larger, her skin is as pale as white rose petals, and her long hair is the darkest black Clara has ever seen. Her lips, tinted crimson, remind Clara of the ropes on the black skyship she had seen the day before.

The pair of fairy girls Clara had noticed at the welcome dance are also candidates, and now that she can see their faces, Clara thinks they must be twins.

The last is an angelican girl with white feathered wings and a dark complexion. She seems to be eyeing the not-quite-elven girl with distaste.

The music starts and Clara directs her attention to the center of the circle where Amor and Madame Rose stand. Madame Rose spins Amor around a few times before stepping out of the circle. Amor stops spinning facing the scaled fae.

He bows to her and she curtsies back. The girl spins and twirls while signing her name. C.E.P.H. The movements seem practiced but only barely memorized.

Through her visits, Clara has learned many dance motions and their meanings but not all of them. She recognizes one of the motions in Ceph's dance to mean swimming, but that is all she is able to decipher.

The girl smiles with pride after finishing, tucking some hair that had fallen loose behind her rounded ear. As she does so, she reveals a set of gills on the side of her neck.

Amor copies her movements, signing her name back at her with the same twirls and flourishes. He then signs his name. It is similar to the pattern he taught Clara but has a few notable differences.

The steps are smoother and more deliberate, and he has changed climbing trees to something else. Clara does not recognize the movement's meaning and wonders what it could be.

Ceph copies his name dance back to him, struggling with a few of the steps. After the last movement, she smiles with an expression of relief on her face and curtsies again.

Clara is glad she didn't have to go first and hopes she will be able to watch Amor's name dance a few more times before it is her turn.

Amor spins around again and lands facing Vira. They bow and curtsy at each other. Clara can't help but notice the smile they share. For some reason, it makes her skin flush and she finds herself balling her hands into fists.

She consciously relaxes her fingers and tries to stay focused as the girl dances her name V.I.R.A. The accompanying motions Clara recognizes mean learning and reading.

Amor signs her name back to her perfectly, as though he has done it many times before, and Clara wonders if she's the girl Amor hosted this pairing ceremony for. He then performs his dance again, but Clara, distracted by Vira's smile, misses the first couple of movements.

Clara watches as Vira performs his name dance back to him with the same practiced perfection, trying to take note of those first few movements. Vira finishes the dance with a wink at Amor and Clara thinks she sees his smile widen.

Clara feels as though she might puke and silently curses herself for feeling anything at all. She purses her lips and tries to remind herself that she doesn't care. That she's over Amor.

Amor spins again, and when he stops he is facing her.

Shit.

He bows to her. She curtsies back and then, with a quick breath, starts her name dance. A broad smile spreads across Amor's face, and his eyes light up with recognition.

He dances her name back at her, mimicking every move perfectly.

Seems she's not the only one with muscle memory from that time. Clara relaxes a little.

She watches carefully, trying to catch the changes as he dances his name again, but this time, those changes aren't there. This time, he dances his name exactly as he had when he taught it to her.

She locks eyes with him as she lets her body repeat the same steps she had remembered that morning. She turns around for the tree sign, and when their eyes meet again Amor smiles at her, his eyes sparkling. Clara returns a gentle smile as she opens her hands like a book.

Relief floods over her as she completes her part of the dance without falling, or missing a step, or something else embarrassing.

Amor continues his turns with the other candidates watching and then repeating their names before dancing his own. Clara tries to keep track of the other girls' names, but her mind keeps wandering.

Why had Amor danced his original name dance with her but none of the other girls? Is it because she hadn't changed hers? Did he know she would remember his original name dance too, even after so long?

When Amor spins and lands facing Stella, Clara breaks from her thoughts. She turns her head and watches as Stella dances her name adding a combination of the two endings she had shown Clara while they were getting ready. Combining them into a new word all her own. Amor pauses for a second before signing "Again Please?"

There is a light chuckle from the crowd of guests, and Stella obliges, repeating her steps. This time, Clara watches Amor as he closely studies Stella's moves, a slight crease between his brows. As she finishes her dance he smiles and repeats her dance back to her, doing surprisingly well.

Clara is certain it would have taken her more than one attempt to copy her sister's name dance. Amor dances his name, and Stella copies it back to him, and then the music stops.

Madame Rose re-enters the circle.

"Wonderful job girls and Amor! Now is the time for Amor to choose the winner of tonight's dance and the first lady who will have the honor of participating in the Passionflower Ceremony." The crowd and the other candidates cheer. "Amor, whose name did you enjoy dancing the most tonight?" Madame Rose asks and the room falls silent.

"I'm going to have to go with a girl who continues to amaze me with her creativity and style," he says before dancing S.T.E.L.L.A and reaching out his hand to her.

Stella squeals with excitement and runs to the center of the circle as the crowd around them claps. Amor places a necklace made of braided wildflowers over her head. Stella dances her name one more time and the crowd cheers.

Clara smiles, enjoying the sheer joy on her little sister's face, but some unwelcome emotion lays over the moment like a fog. Clara tries to push it away, not wanting to acknowledge it.

The music begins playing again, and the circle disperses and mixes, with some guests joining the dance floor and some of the candidates leaving the floor to join their families and friends along the edge of the ballroom.

Stella runs to Clara and throws her arms around her.

"Can you believe it!? I won!" she yells.

"Congratulations," Clara responds, hugging Stella tightly.

They separate and Stella runs off the dance floor toward their mothers waving and showing off her flower necklace.

As Stella pulls away, Clara risks a glance at Amor who is also just separating from a hug with Vira.

Clara purses her lips and quickly averts her gaze. Heat flushes her face as she exits the floor, rejoining her mothers and Stella.

"I'm so happy you'll be able to experience the Passionflower Dance, it really is a life-changing experience," Iris says to Stella.

A young nymph boy, who Clara guesses to be between her and her sister's age, walks up to the four of them. She catches a hint of nervousness in his mannerisms as he approaches.

"Stella? Would you share a dance with me?" he asks, offering his hand to her. The stuttering movement of his indigo wings betrays his attempt at a confident facade. Stella smiles and looks at Clara who nods her head in encouragement.

"I'd love to!" she says, turning back to the young nymph and taking his hand.

Together they walk back onto the dance floor where many other guests have returned.

"My stomach isn't feeling great. I think I'm going to head up to bed early," Clara says to her mothers. It's not a total lie but probably an excuse she would only get away with once.

"Ok, sweetie, drink some ginger tea and lay down for a bit," Iris says. "Come back down and join us if you start feeling better."

"Will do," Clara says. Now that was a lie.

# 7

# The Absence of Time

Clara wakes from a dream steeped in memory, her eyes and pillowcase wet with tears. She sits in her bed for a few minutes still dazed by sleep, longing for a feeling she could barely remember.

She glances at the new time candle on the wall to find that it has not yet lit itself. The sun has not yet risen and most of the fae in Floria would still be asleep.

Back home, there would be tons of fae already hustling and bustling around the city. In Celeste, there was never really a time when the city was fully asleep, but here in Floria, it was so rare to wake before the sun, the fae of Floria did not even track the night hours.

It feels strange to not know what time it is. Back home, the sensation might lead to an anxious tightness in her chest like she's missing something, but here, it feels peaceful. As if time does not exist at all until the sun comes up.

Though sleep calls to her, a quiet walk alone through the halls or the gardens, sounds like exactly what she needs. Before the crowds appear. Before the festivities are back on. Before time begins again.

Clara slips out of bed, quietly dressing in the sweatpants and a tank top she had snuck into her bag after Stella packed it. She slides her shoes on and slowly turns the doorknob, making sure not to make any noise in case someone else is awake.

She cracks the door open, peeking her head out into the shared room. It's empty and dark. She steps through and eases the door closed before tiptoeing across the floor.

Once out in the hallway, Clara breathes easier, her shoulders relaxing and her feet finding their usual rhythm against the stone floor. She passes the stairs, her gaze lingering on them for just a moment before turning away. She pushes past their gravitational pull, resisting the impulse to climb them, and instead sets her mind's intentions on the hedge maze.

Clara exits through one of the back doors of the main house and heads to the maze, breathing deep the sweet, earthy scent of the night air.

Before her first step into the maze, Clara freezes. There's a shadow moving in the darkness; the gentle rustle of leaves. Someone else must have had the same idea she did. She waits, her breath unwilling to leave her lungs. She starts to step away from the entrance but isn't quick enough.

Amor rounds the corner from within the maze, moonlight splashing against his face and as he sees her, he smiles.

"Oh, Hey Clara. I was just thinking about you," he says.

"You were?" The words come out breathy as she's finally able to exhale.

"Yeah. I woke up and couldn't get back to sleep. Decided to go for a walk. I'm guessing it's the same for you?" Amor inquires.

Clara nods.

"Remember when you used to come visit?" Amor asks, taking a small step toward her. "If you couldn't sleep, you would come up the stairs and wake me and we would run through the maze or hang out in the fortress." He looks down at his hands, a soft smile on his lips. "I miss those times."

"Me too," Clara replies, the words slipping out.

"Well then," Amor smiles, looking back up at her. "Race you to the center?" he jests, giving her a sly look. Clara laughs and shakes her head, thinking of all the times she and Amor had done so in their youth.

Clara is unsure if it's the leftover emotions that cling to her from last night's dreams or the sensation of being outside of time, but she feels lighter than she has in a while. Safe and free and unburdened.

"I don't know," Clara says lazily, taking a few casual steps around him and into the maze. "It's kind of early-" At that moment she turns and sprints into the maze leaving Amor behind.

"Hey, no fair" he yells, sprinting off along another path he knows will meet up with hers after a couple of turns.

When they cross each other's paths again, Amor has more or less caught up. Clara ducks into another path that is a little longer but has fewer turns than the one Amor barrels toward.

The air rushes through her hair as she runs as fast as her legs allow and her chest fills with a familiar, childlike exhilaration. It has been so long since she has run for fun.

Clara reaches an opening to the center of the maze to see Amor entering the doorway to her right. They both hurl themselves at the sculpture in the center of the maze, Amor launching himself over the bench standing between him and the statue instead of going around.

Their hands hit the sculpture at the same time. A photo finish with no one to take the picture or call a winner. Just the two of them.

Only now does Clara feel the protests of her body to the sudden activity, and she places her hands on her knees to keep herself somewhat upright. Her breathing is loud as her body tries to take in as much of the night air as it can, but so is his. She looks up to see him leaning against the statue taking in similar huffs of air.

"You got quicker," Clara says between breaths.

"I'm a bit taller now," Amor laughs and presses his hand against his side, taking in another gulp of air. "Longer legs."

"You're not much taller than the last time I visited," Clara replies before realizing they had not raced the last time she was there. The silence hanging in the air told her his mind was following a similar path.

"We didn't hang out much during your last visit, did we?" Amor asks, looking down at his feet.

"No. We didn't," Clara responds. "You were like a completely different person," she adds and Amor cringes at the words.

"I know," he replies, still looking down at his feet. "I was trying to be, well, not myself." His brown eyes meet hers. "I'm sorry."

Clara's chest tightens and she doesn't know how she's supposed to feel. She's held on to her anger from that visit for so long, but were her mothers right? Could they be friends again like they used to be? Does she even want that?

She stands up, her breath steady again, and studies his face. For a moment, she can see her childhood friend hiding just beneath the surface.

Yes, she decides. She does want that. If it is possible.

"It's okay," she finally says, giving him a half smile. "I've just missed my best friend," she adds, averting her gaze.

Amor steps forward and wraps his arms around her. She thinks to pull away, but his embrace is warm and familiar and she gives in to the safety and comfort of this moment.

"I've missed you too," he whispers.

The sun peaks over the horizon turning the sky above them pink and orange. Throughout Floria, candle wicks are sparking to life. Fae are stirring in their beds. Time is turning once more.

Amor releases her and Clara takes a hesitant step back. Silence lingers in the space between them as the sky grows brighter.

"I should go get dressed," Amor says slowly, looking down at his night clothes, "before the guests start waking up." He looks back up at her but stays rooted in place. "I'll see you at the dance tonight?" His eyes search hers.

Clara nods. It's all she can seem to do right now.

Amor smiles, opening his mouth as if to speak again but closes it and swallows. Nodding at her once more, he spreads his wings and flies off toward the third-floor entrance of the main house.

Clara stands in the stillness and quiet left behind in his absence.

As the sun continues to climb higher in the sky, its light kisses the top of the sculpture next to her, reflecting off the silver metal and catching her attention. Clara takes a seat on the bench facing it.

The centerpiece of the hedge maze is always an art piece of some sort, switched out however often. It could be every moon or every year for all she knows, but it is always something new whenever she visits.

The subject of the metal sculpture isn't immediately obvious to Clara. The design is abstract, but as the sky grows lighter the shadow it casts onto the mossy ground calls her attention. The slowly growing shadow resembles a couple embracing.

The feeling of Amor's arms wrapped around her fills her senses again and she closes her eyes, allowing it to seep into her. Time seems to stand still once more, just for a second, but she forces her eyes to open and gets to her feet. Clara turns away from the statue and leaves it behind along with the memories and emotions of that moment.

Maybe they could be friends again, but she can't let herself want more than that. Not again.

# 8

# Trivia Dance

Guests gather on the dance floor as the festivities begin. Excitement buzzes amongst them. It seems the Trivia Dance is a crowd favorite and almost all the guests have packed themselves inside for it.

Clara stands by the punch bowl, sipping on her drink, surveying the party, and eavesdropping on some of the excited chatter. A group of nymphs to her left excitedly speculate on what questions might be asked. To her right a couple of dwarves iron out the terms of a bet based around who can get the most correct answers.

Across the ballroom, Amor stands on a large stage that has been erected in front of the stairs. He's talking with another nymph man who Clara recognizes as one of Amor's old flyball teammates.

Amor nods and the other nymph turns to face the crowd of guests on the dance floor. His dark green, leafy wings lift and spread wide. He motions at the musicians who stop playing and set their instruments into a resting position.

The guests on the dance floor release each other and face the stage. All conversation around the edges of the room quiets as everyone's attention turns to the nymph. He makes a few quick hand signs and then presses his fingers to his throat. When he speaks, his voice projects itself out to the entire room.

"Welcome everyone," the nymph says. His voice is as clear as if he were standing right in front of Clara rather than on the other side of the ballroom. "My name is Tommy and I will be your announcer for the evening," he adds taking a bow. "This is an extra special event for me because Amor here," Tommy says, placing his free hand on Amor's shoulder, "is one of my very best friends. Let's give him a round of applause!"

The crowd cheers and even Clara smiles and puts her drink down to clap. After this morning, she feels more at ease and has actually been able to enjoy her day. She hasn't been dreading the Trivia Dance and even kind of looked forward to seeing Amor again.

"Now, here is how the night is going to go," Tommy says. "I will ask you all a question about Amor and provide you with three possible answers. Music will play for a few moments at which time you will each answer either A," Tommy demonstrates a forward and back dance step, "B," he slides his right foot in a circle along the floor and then does the same with his left, "or C," he spins in a quick circle, "by performing the corresponding dance move. Amor will then show us which answer is correct by performing the move that corresponds to the correct answer. Anyone who gets three wrong answers must leave the dance floor," he says, pacing the front of the stage and motioning out toward the crowd. "The candidate with the most correct answers at the end of the night will win an honorary spot in the Passionflower Ceremony. Are you all ready?" Tommy asks with a rallying cry, and the crowd cheers.

Clara downs the rest of her punch, returning her empty cup to the table before making her way to the dance floor.

"Alrighty then, question number one!" Tommy begins as Clara meets up with Stella on the floor. "What was Amor's first word?"

"Oh easy," says Stella. "Marigold mentions it like every time we visit."

Clara smiles and nods.

"Is it A) mommy; B) daddy; or C) leaf?"

Stella and Clara both spin in circles to lock in their answers.

"I'm seeing some wrong answers out there already," Tommy says "Amor, show the crowd what the correct answer is."

Amor spins around in a circle, smiling out at the crowd of guests.

"C) Leaf is the correct answer" Tommy announces, and a mix of groans and cheers fills the air.

"This might be kinda fun," Clara whispers to Stella, smiling.

"You might even win," Stella jests, nudging her with her elbow.

Clara rolls her eyes and shakes her head at her sister but can't keep a smile from spreading across her face. She looks up at Amor on the stage.

Tonight he's wearing dark brown dress pants with a moss green dress shirt loosely tucked in and partially unbuttoned. He looks very at ease with a large smile on his face and no hint of the nervousness she had seen there the night before.

It might be the good mood she's been in all day or the wine she mixed in with her punch, but Clara thinks, perhaps, winning the trivia dance wouldn't be the worst thing. After all, it wouldn't mean she loves him and wants to bond with him, just that she knows him well.

"Question two. At the age of fifteen, what was Amor's favorite book? Was it A) My Baby; B) The Three Birds; or C) Fly Me To The Moon?"

Clara completes the movement for A before Tommy even finishes listing the answers.

"Are you sure?" whispers Stella. "That was before my time so Imma go with it," she adds. Stella steps forward and back for A as well, and Clara giggles.

"Okay Amor, what is the answer?" Tommy asks and Amor steps forward and back. "The answer was A) My Baby!" Tommy declares.

Stella does a quiet hand clap in Clara's direction and Clara takes a little bow before they both break into more giggles.

"Question three. What catchphrase was Amor known for in his twenties? Was it, A) hello stranger; B) let me tell you something; or C) hey, did you know..."

A few people in the crowd chuckle to themselves including Clara who spins around for C. Stella copies her again.

"Alright Amor, what's the answer?" Amor lifts his foot as if about to do another step but smiles cheekily and spins around. "C) Hey, did you know... is the correct answer," Tommy proclaims, and Clara and Stella high-five.

"Now, if you have gotten all of the answers wrong thus far, I'm going to have to ask you to please exit the dance floor. Those of you still in the game, good job, keep it up. Only seven more to go." At Tommy's request, several fae leave the dance floor.

"Question four. What was Amor's favorite subject in school when he was in his thirties? Was it A) art; B) biology; or C) sports?" Tommy continues.

Stella confidently spins around but Clara shakes her head and slides her feet across the floor making two circle shapes for B.

"What's the answer, Amor?" Tommy asks.

Amor smiles and does the same motion.

"B) Biology," Tommy announces.

Stella gasps. "You were right, Clara. When did he become a jock then?" Stella asks, and Clara shrugs her shoulders.

A fair number of fae leave the dance floor and several of the other candidates leave with them.

"You're on a roll Clara," Stella says. "You haven't gotten a single question wrong."

"Question five," Tommy's voice cuts through. "What did Amor want to be when he was in his forties? A) a marine biologist; B) a writer; or C) an artist?"

Stella steps forward and back for A, falling right into the trap. Clara grimaces at Stella repeating the motion for B.

"Damn it!" Stella says, looking to the stage to confirm her suspicion.

Amor slides his feet, tracing two circles onto the stage. Another wave of people leave the dance floor, including a few more of the candidates.

"The answer is B) a writer. Now, we have made it to the halfway point and we currently have two ladies who are five for five. Clara Glade..." Tommy pauses and the crowd cheers.

Clara's face heats up. Amor locks eyes with her and smiles, looking pleasantly surprised. Clara's face feels even hotter.

"and Vira Nightshade," Tommy continues.

Clara turns to see the red-winged nymph who smiles up at Amor. Amor returns the gesture.

"But it could still be any of these young ladies winning the night so let's keep going. Question six." Tommy's smile drops while he reads the question card and he clears his throat. "What life-changing event happened when Amor was fifty years old?" Was it A) his first kiss; B) his father's death; or C) his first time leaving Floria?" he asks.

"Damn," says Stella. "Mood killer."

Stella and Clara both do the movement for B. When the music stops, Amor does as well and Clara notices that no one leaves the dance floor.

"Pretty sure everyone got that one right," Clara whispers.

Tommy clears his throat "Question seven," he says, "what did Amor spend the majority of his time doing in his sixties? Other than slipping away to the *library* with Vira," he adds, using finger quotes when saying the word "library." He nudges Amor with his elbow and laughs at his own joke.

Amor rolls his eyes. "Very funny, Tommy," he says.

Clara glances at Vira who is laughing and shaking her head. An image flashes through Clara's mind of a kiss on a river bank and she quickly pushes it away.

"Was it, A) studying; B) painting; or C) playing flyball?" Tommy continues.

Instead of letting herself contemplate what Tommy may have been implying, Clara directs her thoughts to the question. The last time she was in Floria, Amor had mentioned being busy with studying and flyball. Those seemed like the most likely answers. She'd never known him to be a painter.

Clara missed almost all of Amor's sixties. The boy she knew before would rather spend his time with his nose in a book, but Amor seemed to have changed so much in those missed years. Stella spins around for C) playing flyball and, with her time almost up, Clara decides to go along with that answer.

The music stops and Amor steps forward and back for A. Studying.

A few other guests and candidates leave the floor.

Maybe he hadn't changed that much after all, Clara thinks, her confidence in how well she knows Amor slightly restored.

"That's three wrong answers for me," Stella says, grabbing and squeezing Clara's hand and wishing her luck before leaving the dance floor.

"Question eight. What was Amor's biggest regret from his seventies?" Tommy asks.

The question pulls Clara's attention quickly back to the stage curious to hear the possible answers.

"Was it, A) missing the first toss at flyball finals; B) jumping into the river to save what he thought was a cat but ended up being a stray clump of sheep wool; or C) not telling his best friend how he really felt about them?" Tommy asks.

Hearing the last possible answer, Clara's eyes dart to Amor. Once upon a time, he had called her his best friend. But Amor isn't looking at her. Had that changed in her absence? She follows his gaze to Vira. Had she taken over the role of best friend? The way they are looking at each other, it seems so.

As the music begins, Vira turns and looks directly at Clara. Their eyes meet for a moment before Clara averts her gaze. With her breath caught in her throat, she looks back up at the stage to see Amor's eyes resting on her.

She's running out of time on this question again, but the answer seems obvious even if the meaning behind the expression on Amor's face is not.

Clara swallows the lump in her throat and spins around. When she finishes her spin she looks hesitantly back at Amor, hoping the questions she wishes she wasn't asking herself aren't plastered across her face.

She doesn't want to know what Tommy was implying earlier, she doesn't want to know when Vira took her place as Amor's best friend.

It doesn't matter. She doesn't care.

Amor holds Clara's gaze for a few seconds before spinning around, recapturing her gaze as he comes to a stop. He half smiles at her.

"C) Not telling his best friend how he felt about them. Aww, I love you too bro," Tommy says, putting his arm around Amor, drawing Amor's gaze back to him and eliciting a laugh from the crowd.

Clara risks a glance over at Vira who is already looking at her, though Clara can't read the nymph's expression through her mask of indifference.

"Question nine," Tommy says, and Clara turns back to the stage. "When Amor was eighty-seven, he published his first book. What was its title?" Tommy asks.

The question catches Clara off guard. She didn't know Amor had published a book. She remembers him starting to write one when they were younger, but he was nowhere near finished. Could it possibly be the same one? She searches her memories for what he wanted to title it.

"Was it A) Sunflowers at Dusk; B) Spice of Life; or C) Tales from my Tree House?" Tommy asks.

That was it! Clara spins for C. After completing the spin she second-guesses herself, thinking he could have just as easily written something else until the music stops and Amor spins around as well.

So he did finish it.

Clara smiles to herself, remembering an image of a young Amor, scribbling wildly in his notebook. The tip of his tongue sticking out of the side of his mouth while he concentrated.

"And finally ladies and gentlemen we have come to the last question of the evening." As Tommy speaks Clara looks around the dance floor to see she, Vira, and the elf-like girl with the pale skin are the last candidates still on the floor.

"As it stands, Vira is in the lead with nine out of nine correct answers, Clara is coming in second with eight out of nine answers correct, and Naomi coming in third with seven out of nine. If we end up with a tie, we do have a few bonus questions to decide the winner, so the game is not over yet," Tommy states.

"Question ten. What are Amor's plans for the future? Does he wish to A) attend University; B) stay in Floria; or C) travel the realm?" Tommy asks.

Clara knows the answer to be C from her conversation with Amor the night of the Welcome Dance and spins in a circle. She looks over at Vira who she assumes probably knows the answer as well. She knew all the others after all.

To Clara's surprise, Vira steps forward and back to answer A.

"Amor, what is the answer?" Tommy asks.

Amor spins around and Tommy announces the answer as C) traveling the world. Maybe Vira didn't know everything about him.

"This means we have a tie," Tommy says "and the winner of the night will be decided by a bonus question."

Clara can feel the excitement of the crowd fill the air around them.

"Clara Glade and Vira Nightshade, I will have you two come to the center of the floor and stand facing away from each other," he says flipping to his last question card.

Clara and Vira both step to the center of the dance floor and Clara can't help but meet her chilly gaze. She tries to read the girl's expression again, but it tells her nothing. When they are just a stride apart, Vira spins around to face away from her, turning her head to the right to look toward the stage.

Clara turns her back to Vira, looking straight ahead to see her sister watching with the other guests. Her sister gives her an encouraging sign and mouths, "You got this!"

Tommy clears his throat and Clara turns her head to see Amor's eyes resting on her.

"Amor had a very impactful conversation this last year that changed the way he viewed love and loss," Tommy says. "Who was it with?"

Clara knows the answer to this question too. Again, Amor had told her the night of the Welcome Dance.

"Was it, A) his mom; B) his teacher; or C) his best friend?" Tommy finishes.

The music starts playing, but Clara can barely hear it over the beating in her chest. The answer is A) his mom.

Amor holds her gaze and Clara feels frozen in place. Would Vira know the answer to this question? If she didn't, Clara could win.

Her stomach fills with rocks as the music plays. She tears her eyes away from Amor and spins in a circle.

When her spin stops she looks at her sister, who is watching with anticipation. Stella meets her gaze with an excited grin.

"So, Amor, What is the final Answer?" Tommy asks.

Clara keeps her eyes on her sister, not wanting to see Amor's face. Not wanting to meet his gaze though she could feel it on her.

She sees the disappointment cross her sister's face as Amor undoubtedly steps forward and back. Stella turns back to Clara with a shrug and a sympathetic smile.

"Which makes the winner of the night Vira Nightshade," Tommy declares.

She must have known the answer after all. Clara hears the click of Vira's heels as she walks up the stairs to the stage. Only then does she risk a glance to see Amor place a braided flower necklace around her neck.

Clara slips off the dance floor and joins her sister in the crowd of guests. Stella hugs her, whispering in her ear.

"You were so close, sorry sis." Clara looks over her shoulder at the door.

"It's okay," Clara says. "I didn't really want to be in the Passion-flower Dance anyway," she adds, pulling back from the hug.

Clara risks another glance up at the stage and locks eyes with Amor. The confusion on his face makes her heart ache. She knew the answer, and he knew that she knew. He had told her the story just two nights ago.

Amor turns, breaking their eye contact to head for the stairs leading off the stage and back onto the ballroom floor.

A knot instantly forms in her stomach. Is he going to come and ask her why she purposefully lost? Right now?

Clara doubted Amor would accept "I don't know" as an answer and that was all she really had for him at the moment.

"I'm going to run to the bathroom," Clara says to her sister, and Stella lets go of her hand. Zigzagging her way through the guests Clara races straight for the nearest door.

# 9

# New Mural

Before she reaches the hallway leading to her room, Clara starts to worry. What if Stella or one of her moms came looking for her? Or worse yet, what if Amor came looking for her? Her room would probably be the first place they would check.

The Welcome Dance made it clear that hiding in their fortress was also too obvious and after this morning, Amor may even go looking for her in the hedge maze. So where could she go?

As soon as she asks herself the question, the answer comes. Second floor. The second floor was mostly guest suites and with luck, no one would think to look for her there. As long as she steered clear of the ballroom balcony, she should be safe.

She turns down a hall and reaches the back staircase, ascending to the second floor. Once there, she walks down the first hallway and turns quickly down another so she is out of sight of the stairs. Clara lets out a breath of relief and sets her back against one of the walls, sliding down it, till she is seated on the floor.

The problem with the second floor is there is nothing to do up here. Though that very fact makes it the perfect hiding spot from Amor, from her mothers, and from Stella, there are no distractions

"

to hide from the memories, and the second her body stills, they catch up with her.

*Clara was peeved at Amor as they waited for his game to start. He had disappeared after leaving the fortress earlier that day, and he barely looked at her during dinner. She couldn't figure out why he was acting so weird.*

*Once the game started, though, her aggravation began to fade. The energy of the Florian crowd was infectious, with songs and chants. And the game was competitive. The visiting team would score, and then Amor's team would score, and soon, Clara felt herself rooting for him.*

*Amor did not disappoint. The first toss of the ball would have him rocketing into the air with quick and powerful wing beats. When the ball was in his hands he would dive, twisting and shaping his wings to precisely direct his fall, ducking and weaving past the visiting team's players. Every time Amor's team scored a point Clara would rise and cheer with the rest of the Floria crowd.*

*She also couldn't deny to herself that Amor looked quite good out there. It was obvious to Clara he was the most skilled flier on his team, and considering how often his teammates passed him the ball, they knew it too.*

*Every throw he made showed off the strength in his arms, and it hadn't escaped her notice that his uniform fit him exceptionally well. As she watched him and cheered, Clara's anger over his unexplained disappearance melted away.*

*After the game Clara, Stella, and their moms made their way to the bottom of the bleachers to meet up with Amor.*

*After some quick congratulations, Marigold recognized one of the other parents in the stands and pulled Aerin and Iris away to meet them. Stella trailed behind the group, leaving Clara with the very sweaty and oddly quiet Amor.*

*They stood in awkward silence for a while before a group of three nymphs around their age descended upon them. Two of the nymphs wore uniforms that matched Amors. One was a girl with light green leaf wings and long brown hair tied up in a ponytail. The other, a boy with sandy blonde hair, tackled Amor as soon as he reached him, his dark green wings wrapping around him.*

*"What a game bro," he yelled. "And all thanks to our MVP!" The boy ruffled Amor's hair as Amor regained his balance.*

*"Thanks, Tommy," Amor says, laughing and pushing the nymph off him.*

*"Great job, Amor," said the other teammate in a soft voice, her eyes glancing up only momentarily before returning to the ground.*

*"I always enjoy watching you play," said the nymph, not in uniform.*

*Her petal wings were bright red and her long blonde hair was braided down her back. She wore a tight shirt that stopped halfway down her torso and a pair of high-waisted pants.*

*"Thanks, guys," Amor laughed again, turning away from Clara to face the group. His wings flared, blocking Clara from the new arrivals like a wall. Clara's heart dropped like a rock into her stomach. Was he trying to hide her from his friends?*

*"I'm gonna go get a drink from the concessions," Clara said, not wanting to continue melting into the background. "Would you like something?"*

*Amor turned back to her as if just now remembering she existed. He folded his wings down so they no longer blocked her from the view of the newcomers. All eyes turned to her, which didn't help the knot growing in Clara's stomach.*

*Her face heated as Tommy looked her up and down but when the scarlet-winged nymph glared at Clara with her sharp, blue eyes, Clara suddenly felt cold.*

*"Na, I'm good," Amor said, holding up his water bottle.*

*"Okay," Clara turned and walked away trying to put distance between them fast.*

*"Who was that? And what's up with her wings?" Clara overheard the red-winged nymph ask.*

*"Oh, she's no one," said Amor, "Just the kid of one of my mom's friends..."*

*Clara couldn't hear anything after that, which she was thankful for. Those words from his mouth were enough to break her. She didn't need to hear more.*

*Clara put on the sweater she had brought with her, wrapping it around her shoulders. She wasn't really cold anymore. Instead, she just felt an odd numbness. She didn't bother sticking her wings through the slits on the back of the sweater as she wandered away through the crowd.*

Clara can't sit still any longer. Instead, she wanders the empty halls, steering clear of the balcony and both sets of stairs.

As Clara rounds a corner, color catches her eye. An unfamiliar mural waits, painted on the wall to her left.

The image is of a tree, growing from a grave. Its roots wrap around the headstone and into the ground below, while its branches reach upwards toward a vibrant blue sky. The headstone is cracked from the embrace of the roots and reads "Here Lies Love."

The largest crack through the headstone cuts right through the middle, separating the i from the e in the word "Lies".

Something about the mural is familiar, but Clara can't quite put her finger on it. It serves as an adequate distraction from the unwanted memories, though. She takes a seat against the wall opposite the mural and examines the brushstrokes, trying to uncover what story may lie hidden beneath the surface.

The loss of a loved one, maybe a husband or a wife, but what is the significance of the tree? Of the cracks in the headstone? Maybe the loved one died many years ago, but their loss is still felt. Or perhaps it's supposed to represent the cycles of life. New life from death and all that.

Clara reflects on the mural until she is certain any search for her has been abandoned, but her mind stays on the twisted vines as she descends the stairs to the first floor. She moves quickly and quietly, not stopping until the door to her bedroom clicks closed behind her.

Clara rushes through her bedtime rituals and crawls into bed. The moment her head hits the pillow, sleep takes her, and she is swept away into a dream.

Some distant voice calls to her, leading her deep into a moonlit forest. The deer path she follows opens out into a clearing and directly in front of her is a familiar tree. Clara knows this tree like an old friend, and she runs to it, throwing her arms around it.

Glancing up into its branches, she is overcome with the sudden urge to climb. Clara positions herself and lifts one of her legs, but as she does so a loud crunching sound hits her ears and she looks down to see a cracked headstone below her feet. Grief and regret swell in her chest, consuming her entire being.

It is then that she wakes.

It takes a moment to remember where she is, and then, leaping out of bed, she quickly dons the sweatpants and shirt she wore the previous morning. The time candle looks as if it has just lit itself as barely any of the wax has melted. Most other fae would only just be stirring in their beds.

Creeping through the room, she slowly turns the knob on her door and sneaks out, past the shared room, into the hallway.

Before long Clara finds herself in front of the mural on the second floor, as if called there by the same voice from her dream. She traces her eyes along the branches of the tree, taking in the shapes and patterns created by the overlapping of its branches.

Clara recognizes this tree. It is the tree she and Amor had started their fortress in. She must not have noticed last night because it's bare without the rope net ladder and sky net in the canopy, but she is now certain it is the same tree.

Why would it be that specific tree in the mural?

"He's a fantastic artist, isn't he?" A musical voice sounds behind her and she turns to see Marigold standing in the hall admiring the mural as well.

"It's beautiful," Clara responds, "but who…" she trails off, turning quickly back to the mural, the answer suddenly obvious. How had she missed it?

"Oh sorry, I assumed he had mentioned it," Marigold says. "Amor painted that a few months ago."

Clara's eyes land on the gravestone. His father's gravestone.

Marigold continues, a solemn look on her face, "I think his father's passing affected him more than I had realized at the time. I was so caught up in my own grief I didn't see him burying parts of himself that day."

Clara stays silent for a few moments, her eyes fixed on the headstone. Amor's words on the night of the welcome dance drift through her mind. The look in his eyes when he talked about the vow he made to himself as his father was buried.

"Here Lies Love," Clara whispers, more to herself, but Marigold nods.

"I wish I had done more to help him navigate that pain, but it seems he has found his way to healing his own wounds," she says.

"I think you did more to help him heal than you realize," Clara states, looking at Marigold and putting an arm around her. The story Amor had told her about their conversation plays through her mind. The words that changed the way he saw love and loss. Marigold's words.

"Thank you, my dear," Marigold says, putting her arm around Clara and squeezing her gently in a side hug. "It is really great to see you again. I know Amor has missed you too. He was so happy when he heard you would be coming."

"Really?" Clara says, a little surprised.

"Oh yes, I hadn't seen him smile so much since..." Marigold trails off with a sad smile.

Clara looks back at the mural, seeing it with new eyes.

A short ways away a door opens and a few guests bustle into the hall.

"I should go check in on the other guests," Marigold says, squeezing Clara's shoulder once before moving past her.

"Mileway dances tonight, see you there," she adds with a smile.

# 10

# Mileway Dance

The garment bag labeled "Mileway Dance" lays on the bed staring up at Clara. She unzips it, immediately taking a step back and withdrawing her hands as if she's expecting a snake to launch itself at her from inside.

She takes a deep breath.

"This is stupid" she whispers to herself, stepping closer to the bed, though she can't quite convince herself to reach for the bag again.

It's just a dress, but it represents something she has been dreading for quite some time. Questions she would no longer be able to avoid.

The Mileway Dances would begin soon and when her turn came, she would be locked in his arms, answering his questions until the mileway was over.

Clara was pretty sure at least one of those questions would be about why she purposefully lost the trivia dance, and as much as she tried to think of a reasonable answer, she still didn't know what she could say that would make any sort of sense to him.

Clara's stomach churns and she has to prompt herself to breathe. Her heart pounds in her chest and her body tells her to run, but her mind reminds her that postponing any longer will only make things worse.

She must face him.

Clara reaches down and pulls the dress out of its protective cover. It is absolutely beautiful. The fabric is a lovely emerald green satin fashioned into a floor-length gown, and for a second, it almost makes Clara forget her worries.

She holds it up against her body and looks at her reflection in the mirror, taking note of the deep V neckline. The knot in her stomach returns, but she pulls the dress on nonetheless.

The straps of the dress are extremely thin and crisscross down her back like the lacing of a corset, leaving the back of the dress mostly open.

Clara gazes at her reflection in the standing mirror and has to admit, she looks stunning.

She can tell immediately this dress was designed by her sister. It fits her perfectly and is eye-catching while remaining simple and elegant, form-fitting, revealing in just the right places, yet extremely comfortable.

The shade of green contrasts well with the lavender color of her wings, somehow making both stand out. Even the green in her eyes looks brighter than normal.

Seeing herself in the dress gives her a flush of confidence, but a glance at the time candle on the wall dispels it with a wave of nerves.

Not all of her nervous hesitation is bad, there's a hint of excitement mixed in. As much as she hated to admit it, the embrace they shared in the hedge maze had been on her mind ever since it happened. If she let herself, she could almost feel his arms around her again, the warmth and safety she felt in that moment. During her mileway dance, she would be in those same arms again. The thought of it makes her insides twist.

She is getting sick of feeling this weird mixture of anticipation and apprehension.

Clara takes a deep breath and steps into the shared room where she is greeted with gasps and compliments from her mothers.

"Do you love it?" Stella asks with excitement at seeing her masterpiece on its intended model.

"Yes Stella, it's gorgeous," Clara replies, sliding her hands down the sides of the dress. "Thank you."

The fabric has a silky satin feel and lays exactly how it should over every curve.

"You really outdid yourself, Stella," Aerin says, making the smile on Stella's face grow broader. "I think it's my new favorite."

"Absolutely gorgeous," Iris says.

"You made yours too, right?" Clara asks and Stella nods, swaying back and forth so the pink satin of her gown's skirt flows around her.

Her dress is strapless with a heart-shaped neckline. The skirt is puffier than Clara's and less form-fitting. Stella looks like a princess and Clara can't help but smile at the excitement on her little sister's face.

"They're both so beautiful Stella," Clara says. "Your skills never cease to amaze."

"Are we all ready to head to the ballroom?" Iris asks.

"Absolutely!" Stella says, spinning on her heels to head out the door without any further delay.

Swallowing her fears, Clara nods and follows.

When Clara steps into the ballroom, the familiar pit forms in her stomach again. She tries to ignore the feeling of so many eyes on her, but one pair catches hers, Amor.

Heat flushes her body as his eyes travel quickly from her head to her feet and back up again. He opens his mouth as if about to continue his conversation with the fae in front of him but pauses.

Though there is a fair distance between them, Clara can make out the words as he finds his voice again.

"Would you excuse me for a moment?" Not waiting for an answer, Amor steps away.

Holding her gaze with his, Amor walks straight toward her. Her mind hums with a single demand; run. But she stays frozen in place until Amor comes to a stop in front of her.

"You look beautiful, Clara," he says, taking her hand and leaning forward to kiss it.

"Thank you," Clara says automatically, distracted by the slight tingle his lips leave on the back of her hand. He looks up to meet her eyes again as he returns to his full height.

"I'm looking forward to our dance," he says with a soft smile.

Clara removes her hand from his, and for a moment he seems not to know what to do with his now empty hand.

"The schedule has you second to last though, so I'm afraid I will have to wait." His smile falters, and he drops his hand back to his side.

"Where do I fall on the schedule?" Stella asks, interrupting the silence.

"You, my dear Stella, are number one," Amor says, shifting his attention. The soft smile returns to his face as he offers her his hand. "Shall we get the festivities started?"

Stella smiles, taking his hand, and the two head to the dance floor. The guests on the dance floor see them enter and some disperse to observe from the sidelines.

Clara watches, wondering if she should be glad she still has some time to figure out what she is going to say to Amor or if the time will just add to her anxiety.

She decides to get a drink.

Next to a large glass bowl of sparkling liquor sits a piece of paper with the schedule of mileway dances for the evening. Clara's name is, in fact, second from the bottom followed by Vira. Of course. The name before her is Charlotte.

Clara thinks back to the name dances and remembers the dance performed by the nymph girl with curly red hair. She scans the ballroom to see if she can find her but quickly gives up on her search.

Clara watches as Amor dances with girl after girl, feeling more anxious as each minute passes and her turn draws closer and closer. It feels like a snake is curling around her body, squeezing her tight so she can only take shallow breaths.

Clara lands on an answer to her earlier question. The waiting is worse.

When Amor extends his hand to the copper-haired Charlotte, her anticipation bubbles over. The snake has wound itself so tightly around her, that she is unable to take in another breath until the bathroom door locks behind her.

Clara leans against the sink and looks up into the mirror, air flooding into her lungs at last. It takes some time for her to regain control of her breathing. When she does, she begins slowing each breath, trying to make them come out smoothly but they shake and stutter.

Turning the faucet to a slow stream, Clara splashes her face with some water. It helps a little. She takes another deep breath, and this time, the exhale leaves her more smoothly. Dabbing her face dry with a hand towel, she takes another.

A light knock on the door causes her to jump.

"Clara? You ok, sweetie?" It's her mother's voice and the sweet melody of it brushes away some of the anxiety.

"Yeah, Mom, I just need a moment," she replies, sounding more confident than she feels.

"Okay, sweetheart," Aerin replies. "Take your time, but it is almost your turn."

"I know. I'll be right out," Clara says.

She examines herself in the mirror, standing up straighter and smoothing a few creases in her dress. Her wings flutter behind her, and she focuses on taking a few more deep breaths, trying to slow their movements.

"I can do this. It's just one dance, and then I'm done. No more ceremonies. Just a guest like everyone else," she assures herself.

Unlocking the bathroom door, she steps out feeling ready to get the dance over with. She grabs her mom's hand, squeezing it lightly, and smiles at her to let her know she is alright. Clara then looks at the dance floor and forces her feet to move.

Clara reaches the edge of the crowd of spectators just as the music begins to fade out and Amor and Charlotte take their final steps. Amor leads Charlotte off the dance floor, searching the crowd before his eyes land on Clara.

He looks back at Charlotte, thanking her for the dance and giving her a brilliant smile and a kiss on the hand. Turning, he walks straight up to Clara holding her in his gaze the whole way.

Clara feels like a deer in faelights, unable to move.

When Amor reaches her, he smiles and offers her his hand.

"May I have this dance?" he asks, his voice low and soft, almost gentile. His eyes search hers.

Clara takes another deep breath and then lightly, hesitantly, slips her hand into his.

Amor leads her to the center of the floor, and she looks around at the crowd of guests watching them.

"Clara?" Amor's voice pulls at her attention and she turns to face him.

"Don't worry about them. It's just you and me," he says, sensing her nervousness. His leafy wings close inward, blocking the on-lookers from her peripheral vision.

Clara looks into Amor's eyes and instantly the crowd disap-pears, but her anxiety persists.

Light, slow music starts to play and Amor lifts Clara's hand in his. Clara lays her other hand gently on his right shoulder.

Amor's chest rises as he takes in a deep breath before placing his free hand on her waist. His fingers wrap around her, gently grazing against the bare skin of her lower back. His fingertips are warm against her skin, but their presence sends a shiver through her.

Amor takes a step forward, pulling her close, and their bodies make contact. Clara's skin heats and she hopes Amor can't tell. In his embrace once more, Clara feels the wall she has built in her mind, between her heart and this nymph, begin to crumble.

She follows his lead, stepping back, side, together, forward, side, together. The tips of his wings brush against the edges of hers every few steps.

They continue their dance in silence, Amor gazing into her eyes. His breath is slow and even.

"Aren't you supposed to ask me questions or something?" Clara asks, wanting to break the silence but internally kicking herself for doing so.

"Right... questions," Amor replies as if he had completely forgotten. "Umm..."

He searches the room for a moment, thinking, and then catches her eyes again.

"Have you been enjoying your time here in Floria?"

That was not at all the question she was expecting. Amor was not usually the type for small talk. Maybe he was warming up for the bigger questions.

"Well," Clara starts, searching for a polite response. "I've enjoyed parts of my visit."

Amor nods, but his eyes wander around the room and he pauses for a moment, his mind preoccupied.

"Did you get my letters?" he asks, not meeting her eyes.

Clara looks at him in surprise. She had almost forgotten about all the letters he had sent after her last visit. The ones she never replied to. The ones that eventually stopped coming. She didn't expect him to ask about them and certainly had not prepared an answer to this question. Should she play dumb? Say, what letters? Lie?

"Yes," she answers truthfully.

Amor meets her eyes, silently asking for more.

"I–" Clara hesitates, swallowing and looking away from him. "I didn't read them though."

He looks away as well, and she spares a glance back at his face to see a wrinkle has appeared between his brows.

"What did they say?" she asks.

Amor breathes in and then sighs, still avoiding her gaze. Clara tries to read his face but with no luck.

"Nothing important I guess," he says. "Not what they should have said, at least."

Clara didn't know how to take that answer.

"What should they have said?" she asks.

Amor looks at her, scanning her face, and Clara wonders what he is hoping to find there. A muscle in his jaw twitches and then he sighs.

"I–" he starts but hesitates, averting his eyes again and swallowing.

"–am sorry," he says with another sigh. "That's what they should have said. That, I know I was a shitty friend to you when you were last here. I pushed you away and I ignored you and I could tell it hurt you, but I did it anyway." His eyes find hers again and he swallows. "I am really sorry."

"You already apologized in the hedge maze," Clara says, not making eye contact. "It's fine."

Amor's grip around Clara's hand and waist tightens.

"Don't say that if you don't mean it," he responds abruptly.

Surprised, Clara can't help but meet his gaze.

"Why do you think I don't mean it?" she asks defensively.

His expression softens as he sighs.

"Well, I mean, last night you seemed to be enjoying the trivia dance, and then." He stops for a moment. His eyes move across her face as if it were a page of a book he's trying to read. "I don't care that you answered wrong. I mean, I was confused, but your sister told me you get stressed about being the center of attention and I figured you probably just didn't want to be in the Passionflower Dance because you'd have to dance in front of everyone, I get that," he said, still scanning her face.

Clara nods.

"But that's not all of it, is it? You wouldn't even look at me after you answered wrong and when I tried to come talk to you, you disappeared," Amor adds. Clara looks away.

"Like that," he says. He rolls his shoulders back and his wings flare slightly. "Why can't you look at me?"

Clara bites the inside of her lip, not knowing how to respond.

"If you're still mad at me, that's fair, I never expected you to just forgive and forget, but don't tell me it's fine then." Amor's tone grows sharp. Clara still doesn't look at him and he lets out another breath, his hold on her loosening. When he speaks again his tone is soft.

"I just mean, I want to really mend things between us and I can't do that if you don't tell me how you really feel."

Clara finally finds the will to look at him. As she opens her mouth to speak, she realizes she can't give him an answer. How is she supposed to tell him how she feels when she doesn't even know?

Amor's eyes search hers and his expression turns to resignation.

"If I wrote you a letter now, like when the pairing ceremony is over and you're back home in Celeste, would you read it?" he asks.

Clara thinks for a moment and then nods.

"Yes," she says. "I," she starts, but the music comes to a halt and Amor steps back, releasing his hold on her waist.

"That felt a lot shorter than the rest," he remarks, looking disappointed. "I'd like to keep talking. Can I find you later?" he asks as he leads her to the edge of the dance floor.

Clara gives a little nod and releases his hand, melting back into the crowd of guests.

Amor turns to face a smiling Vira who offers her hand to him as soon as he is within arm's reach. Her dress is bright red and short, showing off her long legs and matching the red in her wings perfectly.

Clara's chest aches with a mix of emotions she can't name as she watches them glide across the dance floor. Her skin feels cold and exposed, especially the spot on her back where his hand used to be.

Amor and Vira move in perfect sync. Vira is a beautiful dancer. Every step, every hip motion looks practiced and perfected. As they turn, Clara can see the smiles they share and though she can't hear their conversation, it doesn't appear they are at a loss for words.

She sighs, averting her gaze to the floor and closing her eyes for a moment trying to make sense of the feelings swirling through her.

# Letters

Clara heads for the door. She's done trying to sift through her mind for the words that would describe how, and why, and what she is feeling. She's done watching them dance, and smile, and laugh. If Amor really wants to continue their conversation, he can come find her when he's done.

"Leaving early again?" Clara hears from behind her, only a few steps past the door.

She turns to see Stella leaning against the wall, obviously waiting for her.

"I'm just–" Clara starts.

"Running away again," Stella interrupts. "What are you so afraid of Clara?"

"I'm not," Clara starts, but Stella's withering look stops her.

"You are," she says, with no room for argument. "And I bet whatever fear is causing you to flee from the ballroom every night is the same fear that kept you from opening these." Stella reaches into a pocket in her dress and pulls out a stack of envelopes tied together with string. "You can run off, go back to the room, and sit there alone the rest of the night if that's what you really want to do, but at least take these with you." Stella shoves the letters into Clara's hands. "Either open them and read them, or admit to yourself you are afraid of something, and figure out exactly what that is."

Stella turns on her heels and heads back into the ballroom. Clara stands stunned three paces from the door holding the stack of letters and feeling like she was just reprimanded by a teacher and given homework as punishment. Stella has never been quite so blunt, quite so stern, and the short exchange leaves Clara frozen in her tracks.

She looks at the letters in her hands. Amor's letters. But she had thrown them all away. How does Stella have them? Had she been pulling them out of the trash and saving them? They were all still sealed shut. Clara lets out a heavy sigh and stalks back to her room.

Leaning against the closed door, Stella's words spinning through her mind, Clara can't ignore the weight of the letters still grasped in her hand. She lets herself slide down the door until she is seated on the stone floor. Only then, when she is certain the ground won't give way beneath her, does she look at the stack of letters in her hand.

"I'm not afraid," she whispers to herself, but as the words pass her lips she knows they're lies.

Clara groans and then yells, not caring if anyone is around to hear it. She slams the stack of letters onto the ground next to her with such force the string breaks and they splay out across the floor.

She looks at them, biting the inside of her lip and taking a long, slow inhale to calm the raging storm within.

"Fine," she whispers to the letters, picking up the one lying closest to her and reading the date on the stamp. It was sent a month after their last visit.

Clara remembers getting this letter, leaving it on the kitchen counter, making some excuse about having to leave for work, and saying she'd read it when she got home. Of course when she got home to an empty house she had tossed it, unopened, into the garbage.

A few hours later, Stella had returned home and asked her what it said. Clara remembers making up some lie about an apology. Did her sister already know Clara hadn't opened it when she asked, or did she find it in the trash later?

It wasn't that Clara wasn't curious what Amor had to say. In fact, she had tossed and turned for hours that night wondering what was in the letter, but she just couldn't bring herself to go down to the kitchen and read it, because... well, because she was scared of what it would or wouldn't say,

She rips into the envelope and hurriedly unfolds the letter within.

*Hello Clara,*

*My team lost the flyball finals and it was totally my fault.*

*There was a bee flying around the field, and It reminded me of something my biology professor had said about how insects like bees experience the passing of time differently than we do.*

*Like how a bee might see a nymph flying through the air and think that we're flying in slow motion. And then I started thinking about how the trees might experience time. If we were all moving at super speed to them.*

*Well, I got so caught up in the thoughts that I missed the first toss. The other team got the ball and scored before our defense could stop them. We spent the rest of the game trying to make up for it, but we just weren't able to get the lead back.*

*I tried to explain it to Tommy, but he didn't get it. I thought you probably would, though.*

*Anyway,*

*I miss you*

*Amor.*

Clara huffs a laugh. Folding the letter up and setting it down. She picks up another envelope dated a few months later and rips into it, unfolding the paper within.

*Hello Clara,*

*I found an old notebook today. It had a sketch you drew of the fortress in it, along with the book I started writing way back when. I don't know if you remember it. It was called "Tales from my Treehouse."*

*I was thinking, I might try to finish it. What do you think?*

*I hope you are doing well.*

*I miss you,*

*Amor*

She reaches for another.

*Hello Clara,*

*We had a guest art teacher this month and he taught us a class on painting.*

*You know I'm not much of an artist. At least I can't draw like you can, but the painting techniques he taught us were pretty fun and he said I had some talent.*

*My mother got me an easel and some paints for my seventy-fifth birthday yesterday so maybe I'll practice and get really good at it.*

*Also happy almost birthday. Are you doing anything special for it?*

*Anyway,*

*I miss you,*
*Amor*


And another.


*Hello Clara,*
*I know you're probably busy with school or something, but I haven't heard back from you and wanted to make sure you're getting my letters.*
*I would really like to hear from you.*
*I miss you,*
*Amor*


And another.


*Hello Clara,*
*I finished my book, "Tales from My Treehouse."*
*I found a publisher too and I should have printed copies by the end of the year. I'd be happy to send you one if you'd like to read it.*
*I miss you,*
*Amor*


She reads another and another and it feels like catching up on all the missed years. She picks up the last letter, dated about eleven years ago. Her heart aches in her chest as she rips into the envelope.


*Hello Clara,*
*You haven't responded to any of my letters and I know it's probably because you're mad at me, which I get.*

*I was an awful friend the last time you visited. I ignored you and avoided you and pushed you away even though I knew it was hurting you.*

*And then when I started writing to you, I just acted like things were normal, like I didn't know why you weren't responding. I should have said this a long time ago, but I'm really sorry. Please, write back to me. I miss my best friend.*

*I   miss you,*

*Amor*


Tears race down her cheeks as she thinks of how Amor must have felt, never receiving a response to that letter. She wipes the tears away and reads the letter again. As she reads "I miss my best friend," she thinks back to the trivia dance, to that question about his biggest regret.

If she was still his best friend then was he talking about her? If he regretted not telling her how he felt about her, what did that mean?

Then her eyes landed on the next line. Specifically the space after the "I" like he wanted to write something else there but hesitated.

It reminds her of his hesitation earlier when she had asked what should have been in the letters.

"I" he had said "am sorry."

But he also said the letters didn't say what they should have, and this one says it all.

Was there something else he wanted to say?

Her heart whispers an answer and an image flashes through her mind. The last time she had seen Amor before returning home from her last visit. A crumpled letter from Jan, hidden behind her back. Words that she couldn't quite get off her lips.

There's a light flutter in her stomach and her hands quiver. Could he have meant to say "I love you?"

She thinks of the mural and their tree. The way the tree's roots break through the headstone cutting a V-shaped crack through it.

A sense of urgency fills her as she leaves the safety of her room and heads for the stairs. The stairs cannot disappear beneath her feet fast enough, but she finally makes it to the second floor. Down the hallway she runs until she arrives at Amor's mural.

It stares back at her as her eyes trace down the lines of the brushstrokes, following the V-shaped crack in the headstone to where it carefully splits the "i" and the "e".

"Here Lives Love?" she whispers, letting her eyes drift from the roots to the branches of the tree. Their tree. Could it possibly be? That Amor loves her?

Another image flashes through her mind, Amor's face on her first night here, when she asked him if he had found someone he loves. His slight smile as he nodded. The way his eyes rested on her. Could she have been who he meant?

Music from the ballroom drifts to her ears, and she follows it down the hall, finding herself on the balcony overlooking the ballroom. The mileway dances are over and the dancefloor is now full of guests spinning and gliding around in pairs or small groups. Amor's dark curls are nowhere to be found.

"I am not afraid," she whispers to herself, turning to trail along the balcony, tracing her fingers lightly along the railing as she searches for his familiar shape. She comes to the staircase leading to the ballroom below and starts to descend. Glancing up, she finally spots Amor across the ballroom. He's facing away from her, but Clara recognizes the way his hair twists and curls, the shape of his branched horns, and the pine-green shade of his wings.

She reaches the ballroom floor and begins heading in the direction she had seen him. Butterflies fly wildly around in her belly and her heart thuds faster in her chest.

With all the guests between them, she can no longer see him, but as she gets closer, she hears his laugh and follows it. Her breathing becomes short, matching the pace of her heartbeats as she tries to find her words.

"No, no, no," she hears him say, chuckling. "It's not like that. I don't want to bond with her. She's just a friend. She used to have a crush on me a while back, but there was someone else who had my heart."

Clara can see him now. He turns his head to look out across the dance floor. Clara follows his gaze to her. Of course. Vira.

It feels like the floor falls out from under her and she stumbles to a stop. All the air leaves her body and she can't remember how to reclaim it.

Clara's eyes find Amor once more as he turns back to the fae across from him and continues.

"I invited her as a candidate more so she could have the experience. Kind of a gesture of friendship. An apology if you will," Amor explains.

"Are you sure she sees it that way? It seems to me she still has feelings for you," the guest says.

Amor laughs again.

"No, she's over me. When she found out I loved the other girl, well, she didn't talk to me for a while. I apologized and made it pretty clear I wanted to be friends with her but just friends. We've had some good talks since then," Amor says.

Clara's heart drops out of her chest.

She was right from the beginning. Amor just wants to be friends with her. He invited her as an apology, an olive branch, but he loves Vira.

Why had she let herself hope? How could she let herself twist things, read into things, and convince herself he loved her too?

That's it, isn't it? She loves him. Still, and she just wants him to love her back. That's why she was so mad at him, why she didn't want to come, why she couldn't open his letters, why she left the ballroom early every night. Because she was afraid of confirming he didn't love her back.

Suddenly all of the emotions she had been feeling make sense. They have names now, desire, jealousy, hope, and, as her sister said, fear. It wasn't that she didn't know what they were before, she simply didn't want to admit them to herself. Because somehow she knew she would end up here. Heartbroken. Again.

Amor turns and his eyes catch on her. He smiles at her and waves her over, but she turns. Finding the floor again, she starts moving, her sights set on the exit. She needs to get out of here. She needs air. She needs-

"Clara!" Amor yells after her, his voice shattering through her thoughts.

She can hear his footsteps behind her and quickens her pace. She makes it out the ballroom doors. Too late. Amor catches her arm. Clara turns, reigning in the raging sea of emotions filling her chest.

"I read your letters," she blurts out.

"Oh?" Amor says, releasing her wrist and looking at her in confusion. "You brought them?"

"Stella did," Clara answers, taking a step back. "I guess she saved them."

She seems to have surprised him enough to make him forget whatever he was about to say to her.

"I–" Clara starts feeling the reins begin to slip and takes another step backward, "–missed you too, but I..."

She can feel the waves of tears beating at the back of her eyes and she doesn't want to cry in front of him.

"I can't do this right now," she says, turning and running, hoping she can find her way to her room through the tears rolling down her cheeks. Amor yells after her, but she doesn't stop till she finds the familiar door and closes it behind her. She throws herself onto her bed and cries harder than she has cried in twenty-eight years.

Jan was right. This whole trip was a terrible idea.

# Picked

"We've brought some exciting news!" Iris exclaims as she and Aerin enter the shared portion of their suite.

Clara jumps at the sudden entrance, almost spilling the tea she's pouring for herself. Stella looks up from the vanity mirror, the brush paused halfway through her hair.

"It hasn't been announced yet, but Marigold just told us Clara has been selected to dance in the Passionflower Ceremony!" Aerin Says.

"Both of our girls are getting to dance in their first Passion-flower Ceremonies! How exciting!"

"Of course I was," Clara states, cursing her bad luck. "Would you tell Marigold I'm not interested in being her pick? She should give it to someone else."

"Actually," interjects Aerin, "Marigold told us you were Amor's pick."

"What!" Clara turns and looks at her mother incredulously. "That Asshole!"

This was probably him trying to get back at her for ditching out before they could finish their conversation or assuming she would be interested in the "experience". Either way, Clara was fuming.

"Language" Aerin admonishes.

"It's a great honor to be able to participate in the Passionflower Ceremony. I was chosen several times before my own Pairing Ceremony and it was truly life-changing. It helped me learn a lot about myself. Even if you don't want to bond with Amor, this could be a great experience for you," Iris persuades.

"Are you *that* against the possibility of exploring your feelings with Amor? You two used to be inseparable. What happened?" Aerin pushes.

"We changed," Clara spits out, slamming down her teacup before storming out of the room.

Clara stomps down the hallway, glancing over her shoulder once to ensure she is not being followed. Thankfully, it seems her mothers know better. She continues out into the garden, her stomach filling with rocks and her face starting to heat.

Why did he pick her? She takes a left and runs into the hedge maze where she won't be found, at least until she can get her emotions under control. Her mother's voice echoes through her head, *"You two used to be inseparable, what happened?"*

*Clara got her soda from the concessions and then found her moms in the bleachers, chatting with Marigold and a few other adults. Not long after she joined them, Amor came running up.*

*"Mom, the guys and I are gonna go hang out on the riverbank to celebrate, Cool?" he said quickly as if already knowing it was in fact "cool."*

*"Sure, bring Clara, I'm sure she'd love to meet your friends," Marigold answered.*

Clara had not cared to spend any more time with his friends and was going to say so before...

"I don't think Clara would enjoy it, it's mainly gonna be -"

"I'd love to," Clara had cut in before she could stop herself. She really hadn't wanted to go, but something about Amor speaking for her just made her want to contradict him.

"Me too! Me too!" exclaimed Stella.

"I don't know Stella," said Aerin.

"It's Okay, I'll look after her if she wants to come," Clara interjected, hopeful there would be at least one person, other than Amor, she knew there.

"Well ok, but you have to stay with your sister. No running off," Aerin agreed.

"Fine," said Amor.

"Yay!" exclaimed Stella.

As the sun started to set, Clara and Stella followed Amor to the stream where several small bonfires had already been lit. Next to one of the bonfires, drinking bottles of beer, were the three nymphs from before. There were another fifteen or twenty nymphs who all looked to be between the ages of seventy and one hundred scattered along the bank of the river. Some were in uniform, others not. They all huddled around the bonfires.

As she noticed Amor walking up to the first bonfire, the flirty girl hopped off the log she was sitting on and grabbed another beer from the cooler by her feet. She pranced up to Amor who was a few paces ahead of Clara and Stella and threw her free arm around Amor's shoulder, turning her back to the two girls. She handed Amor the beer before not so quietly whispering "What are they doing here?"

"I'll tell you about it later," he whispered back, taking the beer and cracking it open.

*Tommy was lying in the sand by the cooler. As the girls joined the others by the bonfire, he reached into the cooler and pulled out another beer, offering it to Clara.*

*"No thanks," she said.*

*He motioned to Stella.*

*"No, She's only sixty," Clara said quickly.*

*"Hey, I started drinking at fifty and I'm fine," he said "Let her decide for herself."*

*Stella glanced at her sister and then back at the guy pointing the beer in her direction.*

*"No thank you," she said.*

*Amor had wandered off with the flirty girl, so Clara turned back to Tommy.*

*"Got any non-alcoholic drinks out here?" she asked*

*"Yeah, I think the cooler for lame people is over there somewhere." He pointed further down the stream to one of the other bonfires.*

*Clara rolled her eyes, took Stella's hand, and walked over to the next closest bonfire. Sure enough, the cooler there had some bottles of water. She handed one to Stella and grabbed one for herself.*

*Music drifted up from a speaker stationed near the next bonfire down, and Stella pulled on Clara's hand.*

*"Can we go dance?" she asked.*

*"No one else is dancing," Clara pointed out.*

*"SO?" Stella Implored "Maybe they're all just waiting for someone else to dance."*

*Clara rolled her eyes. "Fine."*

*Stella dragged Clara over to the speaker and then started spinning around her head cast back and her face bathed in the moonlight. Clara smiled; at least Stella was enjoying herself. Glancing around, she spotted Amor and the flirty girl seated around the first bonfire.*

*"Clara, dance" demanded Stella.*

*Clara complied and the two of them danced together until their legs got tired, and they laid down on the ground to catch their breath.*

*"I'm sleepy," Said Stella.*

*"Me too, are you ready to go back to the house?" Clara asked, brushing some hair over Stella's pointed ear to keep it out of her face.*

*Stella nodded her head.*

*"Okay, Let's find Amor and tell him we're heading out."*

*Clara stood up and looked around for a bit before spotting Amor and his clique, chilling at the same bonfire as before. As she and Stella neared the group, Clara could hear laughing and parts of the conversation.*

*"-look so stupid dancing around like that. What idiots," said the flirty girl and the rest laughed, including Amor.*

*"The older one seems to have a crush on you too, always looking over in your direction," said Tommy.*

*Then Amor's voice. "Yeah, it's like she's in love with me or something."*

*They all laughed and Clara stopped, her feet cemented to the sandy ground. The thudding in her chest grew so loud it almost blocked out their laughter ringing in her ears.*

*"Hard to blame her," said the flirty girl, putting her arm around Amor, and turning his face toward her, kissing him.*

*Clara's heart shattered and she stood frozen in place, hesitant to move a muscle lest the rest of her shatter too.*

*Stella looked up at Clara.*

*"Let's just go back to the house," she said. Clara complied, but the laughter continued to bounce around in her head long after they had re-turned to the main house.*

Clara sits in one of the maze's dead ends with her knees tight to her chest and her head cradled in her crossed arms, trying to steady her breathing. As she breathes she thinks of that night twenty-eight years ago, the laughs still echoing in her ears. Amor's laughs from the previous night bleed into the memory.

The rocks in her stomach turn to hot coals and she stands, marching out of the maze, into the house, and up the stairs, straight for Amor's room.

Bam Bam Bam. She hammers on his door as hard as she can. He opens the door, his shirt unbuttoned and his curly hair ruffled on his head, clearly in the midst of getting dressed. A bright smile lights his face, but her anger only boils over. Clara pushes past him into his room.

"Where the fuck do you get off picking me for the Passion-flower Ceremony?" she spits out.

"You're mad?" he says, obviously confused. His wings dropped to his sides, the tips of them skimming the floor "I thought you-"

"What? You thought I would enjoy the experience or some-thing? I told you I didn't want to dance in front of everyone."

"Well actually, I suggested that. You haven't really told me any-thing," he cuts back, a pinch of anger and frustration in his words. "I've been trying to ask you how you feel, but you barely speak to me and then you just disappear."

"I don't know what you want me to say," Clara replies, folding her arms over her chest.

"I want you to tell me how you feel about me," Amor blurts out.

"How I feel? You want me to say I'm in love with you or some-thing?" Clara scoffs.

"Only if it's the truth," Amor says, his voice getting quiet and his eyes frozen on her.

Silence lingers between them for a moment.

"Why would I love someone so arrogant and big-headed and conceited?" Clara sneers, turning away from his gaze.

"Aren't those all the same thing?" Amor probes.

"Oh FUCK OFF!" Clara shouts over her shoulder, throwing her arms in the air. "You are not going to embarrass me like this. Un-pick me" she demands.

"I can't, my mom already gave the picks to Madame Rose to start sizing the dresses. What's your problem?" Amor shoots back.

"You're my problem! I didn't even want to come here, but Stella convinced me and now I'm going to have to put on some frilly dress and dance around like an idiot for what? For the 'experience.'" Clara says pacing Amor's room. She turns, closing the distance between them. "You wanna know how I feel about you, Amor? Fine, you're an asshole and I hate you."

Clara starts toward the door.

"Well if that's how you feel then just drop the flower the second it touches your fingers and be done with it!" he yells at her, his wings raised.

Clara turns to look at him one more time as she steps past the threshold of his bedroom.

"I intend to," she spits out, slamming the door behind her.

The chatter in the shared room hushes as Clara storms in. Her mothers stop talking to watch her, Iris starts to open her mouth, but Clara puts her hand up to block the words before they leave her mother's lips. She does not slow until she is on the other side of her bedroom door. Safe.

As soon as the door slams shut behind her she thrusts herself onto the bed and lets out all the churning emotion, screaming into a pillow.

A soft knock at her door, after only a moment or two, makes her stop.

"WHAT!?" she roars.

The door squeaks open and Stella steps in.

"Are you okay?" Stella asks in a small voice.

"Yeah, I'm fine, he's just so infuriating. I mean what a dick, right?" Clara implores, looking for some backup.

"I mean..." Stella hesitates "If you are talking about the things he said the last time we were here, then yes, he was totally an arrogant asshole," she offers using the words Clara shouted at Amor. Had her sister overheard some of their conversation?

"But..." Stella continues, "Well, you said it yourself, Clara, you've both changed, and in the whole time we've been here, all I've seen from Armor is kindness and respect. Maybe he's not that guy anymore, and maybe you should give him another chance?"

"Not that guy anymore? Ha!" Clara laughs humorlessly. "If he's so changed then why would he pick me for the Passionflower Ceremony? Huh? He knew I didn't want to take part and I mean, the gall to think I'd still have feelings for him-"

"Did you ever think maybe he picked you because he has feelings for you?" Stella interrupts, her patience clearly wearing thin. "You may not see how he looks at you, but I do."

Clara rolls her eyes. "He doesn't have those feelings for me. He just sees me as a friend and always has. He's in love with that other girl. Vira. I heard him say it."

Stella looks confused. "Are you sure? I'm rarely wrong about these things."

"I'm sure. I mean, he didn't say names, but it was pretty clear who he was talking about," Clara says.

An image of the smile on Amor's face the moment he opened the door to see her flashes through her mind. The smile that had fallen to confusion as she pushed past him. It wasn't mocking or amused. It was kind and genuine. Could she have misinterpreted Amor's words last night?

She shakes the image from her mind. She's not doing this to herself again. Every time she gets her hopes up, she ends up with a broken heart. No more.

"If you want to drop your flower tonight that's totally up to you," Stella says. "But if you still have any positive feelings left for Amor, and I think you do, you owe it to yourself to explore those. Otherwise, you might do something you'll regret for the rest of your life."

With those last words, Stella turns on her heel, leaving Clara alone with her thoughts and memories.

# 13

# Her Passionflower Dance

Clara and the other girls participating in the Passionflower Ceremony spent the rest of the morning with Madame Rose as she walked them through the movements of the dance.

Clara already knew them, but the reminder was helpful, though, she could have done with just a few run-throughs. It's not like she was going to be dancing the whole thing anyway.

Vira was, of course, perfect on every repetition. Stella remembered some of the moves, and what she didn't remember, she caught up on quickly. Beatrice and Naomi, who were picked by Marigold, didn't seem to have any previous knowledge of the dance. They were the only ones really who needed to spend the whole morning practicing.

After lunch, they had fittings for the traditional dresses, and as their hems were pinned and their waists were pulled in or let out, the other girls talked. They talked about how excited they were to be a part of the ceremony, about how they met Amor, and about how their mileway dances went. Clara did her best to tune them out.

When Beatrice asked her specifically how she and Amor had met, she simply replied, "Our mothers are friends."

Stella had given her a look but didn't say anything.

Once the seamstress was done with them, they were sent to Mr. Holly who introduced himself as one of the nymphs who raises and cares for the Florian passionflowers. He then lectured them on the history of the Passionflower Dance and what effects they could expect from their contact with the passionflower venom.

Primarily burning sensations and mild hallucinations. Fun.

After that, they met with Madame Rose again who showed them their blocking for entering the ceremonial circle. And finally, they were sent off to have dinner and get dressed for the ceremony.

As she fidgets with the skirts of her dress, Clara wishes for the day to be over already. The moonlit sky above her assures her it almost is, but there is one more thing that must be done.

Clara and the other four women begin walking single file toward the ceremonial circle at the center of town. They are dressed in their matching white tulle dresses. The park around them is adorned by the light of the almost full moon directly above and millions of white candles line their path.

Looking ahead, Clara can see the guests forming a large circle around the ceremonial pavilion surrounded by another vast array of candles.

Stella leads the line followed by Vira, Beatrice, Naomi, and lastly, Clara.

As Stella approaches the circle of guests, they part in front of her, allowing them to continue forward, onto the golden pave stones at the center of the circle.

Moonlight and candlelight mix, reflecting off the surface of the crystal-clear water in the pool that sits in the middle. Encircling the pool are five pedestals, evenly spaced about five feet away from the central pool.

Perched on each pedestal sits a fiery red flower with long purple tendrils hanging down into a small bowl of water.

Clara scans the crowd nervously as she steps onto the pave stones. The full ballrooms of the previous dances had felt crowded. Now, with all of the guests gathered around the ceremonial circle, it seemed the crowd had doubled in size. Butterflies try desperately to escape Clara's belly and she purses her lips together to hold them in.

Stella confidently leads the line, turning to walk in a circle past each of the pedestals until she reaches the one closest to where they had entered.

The other girls follow behind, stopping at their assigned pedestals, leaving Clara at the last pedestal between Stella and Naomi.

As she waits in her designated spot, she can't help but scan the crowd in front of her. To her left are her mothers, giving her and Stella big smiles and encouraging gestures. Three rows back, directly in front of her, Amor stands next to his mother.

Though the paved circle Clara and the other girls are standing on is flat, the grassy ground surrounding the circle is sloped upwards allowing the people in the back rows to be seen over the heads of those in front of them. Amor smiles as he talks to Marigold before he locks eyes with Clara for a brief moment and his smile wavers.

Madame Rose glides onto the paved circle, arms spread wide as if stepping onto a stage.

"Welcome everyone! To the fifth night of Amor Aiday's pairing ceremony," she announces with a gesture to the crowd. "Allow me to introduce the five ladies, who will be performing the Passion-flower Dance tonight."

The whimsical nymph continues gliding over to stand near Stella. "Stella Glade, from Celeste, was chosen on the second night by Amor for her creative name dance," she says, putting her hand out.

Stella takes Madame Rose's hand and curtsies as the crowd cheers. As the cheers subside, Madame Rose drifts over to the next pedestal.

"Vira Nightshade, from right here in Floria, won her place on the third night by getting the most correct answers in the trivia dance," Madame Rose continues, and the crowd cheers again as Vira takes Madame Rose's hand and curtsies.

Madame Rose continues around the circle stepping between the other two girls.

"Traditionally, each parent gets a pick for the Florian Passion-flower Dance, however, since Amor's father is not able to be with us today, Marigold has chosen two girls for tonight's dance."

Clara turns to look at Amor. She is not the only one. Amor looks down in a failed attempt to escape the glances and the accompanying sympathy for the loss of his father. Marigold puts her arm around him, pulling him close and he peeks up at her. They share tight smiles of understanding.

Madame Rose continues, extending both hands to the girls on either side of her.

"Marigold has chosen Beatrice Thirsten from Dioran, and Naomi Cathridge from Halmsdale."

The girls take her hands and curtsy as the crowd cheers their attention, returning to Madame Rose.

As the crowd's gaze shifts away from Amor, he relaxes, his shoulders drop slightly, and he catches Clara watching him. He gives her a half-hearted smile before her attention is pulled away by the approach of Madame Rose who extends a hand to her.

"And finally, we have Amor's pick, Clara Glade, from Celeste." Clara places her hand in Madame Rose's and curtsies, tilting her head down as she does so.

When she looks up, she meets Amor's gaze, and he mouths "I'm sorry."

Little late for that.

Madame Rose releases her hand and glides to the center of the circle in front of the round pool.

"For millennia, we have lived alongside these beautiful and fierce flowers. When our ancestors came here from the birth realm, they brought the seeds with them and planted them along a lake deep in the forests," Madame Rose says, capturing the attention of the crowd.

"When our histories were taken from us, the passionflower venom gave us truth. When we were consumed by hate and vengeance, the passionflower venom gave us love, and with that love, we regained our freedom." As she speaks, the older nymphs in the crowd bow their heads, many closing their eyes and placing their hands against their chests.

"The Passionflower Dance is a celebration of that truth, love, and freedom. The venom may cause pain, but those who are brave enough to dance with the flowers will always find truth."

Madame Rose shifts her attention from the crowd to the dancers, locking eyes with each girl as she continues.

"Any who are able to complete the dance and place their flowers in the center pool, most certainly have love," she says, and her gaze falls on Clara. "May that love bring you freedom."

Madame Rose glides to the edge of the circle to join the rest of the crowd and flicks her wrist at the musicians.

Clara looks down at the flower in front of her as the music begins. She picks up the passionflower with her right hand, and the purple tendrils wrap around her fingers and forearm. The venom from the flower burns at her fingertips as she begins the first steps of the dance.

She thinks about opening her hand to drop the flower to the ground, but her sister's last words to her the previous night stand stubbornly in the front of her mind.

Clara slowly moves through the first steps of the Passionflower Dance and soon, her mind is adrift, whisked away across the sea of emotions flowing through her. It feels like time is decelerating as her body continues to twirl and spin in slow motion.

The rest of her is somewhere else, lost in a vision. The intense burning sensation climbing up from her fingers, the only thing tying her to the present.

*"Careful, Clara!" Amor yelled from the base of a tree. He looked so young even with a wrinkle forming between his brows.*

*"Stop being such a worry wart, Amor, I'm fine!" Clara's voice drifted to her ears, even though she hasn't spoken. Tilting her head, she follows the sound of her own voice and finds herself looking up at a younger version of herself.*

*She was thirty-something, straddling a branch eight or nine feet from the ground. Little Clara pressed forward into her hands, lifting her hips and swinging a foot underneath her body.*

*The sting of the venom covers Clara's palm.*

*Looking up, the younger Clara tossed a rope over another branch above her and wrapped it tightly around her forearm.*

*The burning sensation continues to spread up her wrist and around her forearm.*

*Little Clara leaned into the rope to steady herself as she stood up, placing her other foot in a good foothold.*

*"See, I'm fine," she yelled back down to the ground.*

*Amor let out a breath as little Clara readjusted the rope and started tying a knot.*

The fire continues to climb Clara's arm into her shoulder, but she pushes the sensation to the back of her mind, focusing her attention on the little girl in the tree.

She remembers this day and she flinches before it happens.

*Some bark broke away under little Clara's foot and she fell, grabbing for the branch below. Her chest hit the branch first and knocked the wind out of her.*

The flames begin to lick at Clara's chest, radiating through to her shoulder blade.

*Little Clara's small wings flapped hard and fast, but they did not slow her fall. She hit the ground.*

The burning ignites Clara's rib cage and the side of her head.

*Amor raced over to the young girl in a panic.*

Ignoring the pain, Clara follows him.

*"Clara! Are you ok?" he asked, dropping to his knees and scooping her head up into his lap. "Clara?"*

*His face went white when he was met with silence. Amor removed his hand from under her head, seeing the scarlet blood left there.*

*He started breathing fast.*

*"No no no no no," he whispered under his breath. "Clara, wake up!"*

*Tears started to fill his eyes and he wiped them away, turning and looking at the sled they had used to bring the pile of ropes from the main house.*

*Gently, Amor laid Clara's head back on the forest floor and ran over to the sled, clearing it in a swift motion before pulling it back to little Clara, as she lay motionless on the ground.*

*He looped his left arm under her neck and the other under her knees lifting her onto the sled and laying her down as carefully as he could.*

*"I'm going to get you back to the main house and Dr. Calen will heal you. Don't worry," he said, more to himself.*

*Clara watches as his expression turned from fear to determination.*

*Amor grabbed the rope tied to the sled and started pulling her back to the main house.*

*Clara chases after them disregarding the bite of the flames as they continue into her neck and face. As she races after the pair, the burning extends down to her hip.*

*The scene morphs and darkens, and a cool sensation surrounds her, soothing the pain in the right side of her body. When her eyes adjust, she is looking down at her younger self lying in a bed in the medical wing.*

*The room was lit primarily by the moonlight shining through the window. Amor slept, slouched over in a chair next to the bed. There was a rip in one of the knees of his pants and both were wet and muddy.*

*"Amor," she hears herself say from the bed.*

*Clara turns to look at the young girl and she can see by the way she looked at him that she was falling in love for the first time. She hadn't realized until now that this was the moment the friendship she felt for him had become more. From here on, that love grew. And though she'd been hurt, Clara could recognize the same love still there in her heart.*

*It was crystal clear now, she loved him. Maybe he didn't feel that way about her. Maybe he felt that way about someone else. But at that moment she knew if she didn't tell him, if she kept denying those feelings, she would regret it for the rest of her life.*

*Clara looks back at the little boy as his eyes fluttered open and he jumped from his seat. As he smiled, hugging her, tears streaking down his cheeks.*

*He deserves the truth too.*

Her vision blurs and she blinks to clear it. When she does, she sees water rippling around the Florian passionflower and her hands resting in the center pool. The searing ache fades as the cool water washes away the last of the venom. Her right hand is dyed bright red and red streaks branch their way up her arm.

The ripples in the pool settle and she can see the reflection of her face. The red streaks continue up the right side of her neck and onto the side of her face. They are beautiful in a way. A red tear slips from her eye, running down her cheek and falling into the pool.

Clara looks up at the crowd. Stunned eyes locking on hers, his eyes, nothing but surprise on his face.

She can't blame him. Less than twelve hours ago, she had told him to fuck off and called him names. She had told him she hated him. Her head pounds with regret.

Clara has some explaining to do, but for the first time, the thought of doing so doesn't fill her with dread or anxiety, just resolve.

She has to tell him how she really feels, but there are so many fae standing between the two of them.

Before she can move another muscle, her mothers are by her side wrapping a silk sheet around her and leading her from the garden.

Her mind spins. What is she going to say to him? How is she going to explain how she feels? How is she going to apologize for what she said that morning?

Her mothers are talking, but Clara's brain isn't processing their words. As far as she is concerned, they could be speaking gibberish. They lead her to her room and sit her down on her bed.

"She's not in the mood to talk, Iris, you remember what it was like. Let's give her some time to process," says Aerin.

"You're right. Get some sleep if you can, Clara. We can chat in the morning," Iris agrees.

Her mothers leave the room, closing the door behind them and leaving only silence. Clara lets herself fall backward onto the bed. Everything after seeing her reflection in the pool is a blur and her mind reels from all the memories and emotions the venom awoke.

# 14

Wardrobe

Clara lays in bed staring at the ceiling for so long that she completely loses track of time. She tries closing her eyes several times to see if she can drift off to sleep, but the memories swimming through her head are just too loud. Instead, she stares at the wood and stone ceiling above her bed until there is a knock at the door.

No, not the door. Turning her head on the pillow, she follows the sound to where it came from: the wardrobe.

"Pssssstt, Clara, it's me," came Amor's voice from the direction of the wardrobe. The noise in Clara's head suddenly halts, and she flies out of bed, throwing open the wardrobe. Nothing but her garment bags greet her in the cramped interior.

"I'm behind the wardrobe. You'll have to push it aside," Amor's voice came again.

The wardrobe is heavy, but it moves without too much effort. Clara slides the wardrobe across the floor to reveal Amor, standing in a dark passageway.

"I hope I didn't wake you," Amor says.

"No, I couldn't sleep," Clara replies.

"Same. I needed to see you. Before tomorrow." There's urgency in his voice. He rubs his thumb over the back of his other hand.

"Well, come on in," Clara says, stepping out of the doorway to let him through.

As he passes her, she leans into the passageway to see the long hallway parallel to her bedroom wall.

"How long has there been a passageway behind..." she starts to ask but decides it's a question for another time when Amor grabs her hand.

She turns to see him staring down at her bright red skin. That same wrinkle between his brows as that day in the woods had formed. His eyes trace the red up her arm, up her neck, to the right side of her face. He reaches forward with his hand as if to touch the lines on her cheek but stops short.

"Did it hurt?" he whispers, eyes examining the red designs.

"Not too bad," she lies, but when his eyes meet hers, inspecting them deeply, she adds more truthfully. "Not anymore."

"Why?" His eyes lighten, and he clears his throat. "Why didn't you just drop the flower?" he asks, dropping his hand back to his side, suddenly seeming to remember it was hanging in the air next to her face.

"Because..." Clara starts.

Shit.

She thought she would have more time to come up with a coherent answer. She had started working through some opening lines in her head, but they were gone now. Cleared out by his intense gaze. Clara turns and takes a few steps away from him, her mind awash in emotion, otherwise, utterly blank. Amor's letters, crumpled in the corner of her room catch her eye and suddenly three words are all she can think of.

"I love you," she says turning back to him.

Too late to take it back now at least.

He exhales quickly like the air is knocked out of him by some unseen force, a surprised expression washes over his face, the same one he had when she had looked up at him from the pool. The silence stretches on for what feels like decades.

"I know I said I... I didn't mean to..."

Clara's brain sprints to come up with some explanation, but there are too many streams of thought to make sense of any one, like her brain is trying to catch up from its momentary lapse.

Amor inhales as if he has been starved of air for days and he closes the distance between them in three long strides. Wrapping an arm around her waist, he pulls her to him. Tenderly, his hand slides across her cheek, under her hair, and curls behind her head. Before she can organize her thoughts, his lips collide with hers. He kisses her deeply.

A cloud of warmth and ecstasy surrounds her and as his lips leave hers, she realizes her brain has gone completely blank again.

"I'm so confused," he says, closing his eyes and resting his forehead against hers. "Happy, don't get me wrong, but–"

"I know. I..." Clara hesitates for a moment before she pulls her head away prompting Amor to look up.

"Wait, I'm confused too," she says, shaking her head. Her hand moves to rest on Amor's wrist as she looks up into his eyes.

"You love..." she starts, but the words are stolen away by doubt.

Amor smiles.

"I love you too," he says.

"But Vira." The words leave her mouth before she can stop them.

"Is just a friend," he says, shaking his head slightly. "You thought I loved her?" His brow wrinkles again.

"Well, yeah." Clara thinks that should be an obvious assumption after the past several days, but Amor still looks confused.

Clara sighs. "Do you remember the bonfires by the river?"

He nods, the crease between his brows cemented in place. Clara steps back, breaking the contact between them, and sits on her bed.

"I overheard what you said to your friends, and I saw Vira kiss you," she says.

Amor takes a seat next to her.

"What did I say?"

"I guess it was mainly them saying things. But you laughed." Clara glances at him and finds his eyes pointed at the floor. "And then Tommy said he thought I liked you, and you said–"

"It's like she's in love with me or something," Amor finishes for her, clenching his fists. Amor shakes his head.

"I'm so sorry. I was trying to deny a lot of things back then, a lot of emotions. I was trying to fit in. I know it's not really an excuse."

Amor turns to face her.

"When you came back to Floria after so long, when you pulled me to the fortress, when you looked at me the way you did, I..." he hesitates, lifting his eyes to the ceiling overhead as if searching for the answer there. "I felt something I hadn't in a long time. Something I thought was gone, and it scared me."

Amor's eyes turn glossy, and tears brim, hovering on the edges of his eyelids, but he blinks them away.

"I'm sorry I hurt you. The truth is, I knew I loved you then, but I didn't want to risk the pain that could come from admitting it."

Clara felt a weight lift from her chest as the events of that visit began to make sense. She could relate to his fear, his hesitation.

"I'd been afraid of love ever since losing my father, and when we were up in our fortress, and you looked at me like that, I knew what I felt for you. It scared me, and I ran. When I said that at the bonfire," he takes a breath, and his gaze turns distant as he remembers the moment, "It's like she's in love with me or something, it was the first time I really thought you might actually love me back."

A slight smile flickers over his features.

"Which scared me even more, the thought of you going through what my mom did. And then Vira kissed me and it felt safe. I convinced myself that ignoring the love I felt for you was safer, for both of us. So I kept avoiding you and pushing you away."

Clara listens, breathing slowly as she experiences the story of her first heartbreak through his eyes.

Amor reaches out for Clara's hand and she reaches back, placing her hand in his and squeezing lightly.

"After that, I looked around and didn't see you, so I figured you had already gone back to the house. I didn't know you heard or saw any of that. I'm sure it hurt."

Clara nods.

"I'm truly sorry, Clara. If I could go back, I'd–"

"It's okay," Clara says, and this time she means it. "I guess I've been doing the same thing. Not letting myself admit how I felt so I wouldn't have to risk the pain of finding out you didn't love me back."

She looks down at their clasped hands.

Amor lifts his free hand to tip her chin, gently redirecting her gaze back to his face.

"I have loved you for as long as I can remember, and I'm not afraid of that anymore," Amor says. "I love you, Clara."

"I love you too," Clara says, leaning forward and pressing her lips against his.

He smiles against her mouth, lifting his hand and intertwining his fingers in her hair. His thumb brushes lightly across her cheek, catching a tear she hadn't realized was there.

# 15

❧

# The Talk

Clara awakes to bright light pouring through her window and hushed voices on the other side of her door. Though sleep pulls at her she sits up. The time candle shows a few hours have already passed since sunrise.

She blinks slowly still in a daze from sleep. She didn't even remember falling asleep.

Could it all have been a dream? Clara turns to face the wall where the wardrobe once stood, where the passageway had been.

Had been, because it was no longer there.

Clara jumps out of bed and races to the wall, placing her hand on the cold stones. She pushes on them and they remain solid. She pounds her fist against the hard stones and her heart sinks to the cold floor.

The wardrobe was pushed aside though. Did she move it in her sleep? Maybe she had hallucinated Amor's visit last night. She looks down at her right hand, her skin a deep crimson.

Had Amor really come to see her or was it all just another vision from the passionflower venom?

Clara brings her fingers to her lips. His kisses had felt so real. She runs her fingers through her hair, trying to recreate the feeling of Amor's tangled there. His touch felt so real. But her visions in the ceremonial circle had felt real too.

She drops her hands. She needs to find Amor and talk to him. If last night was all a dream, she needs to tell him how she feels all over again.

Somehow she doubted his answer would be the same. Her stomach starts to knot up and she shakes herself. If she thinks too far ahead into her day, it may leave her frozen, so instead, she resolves to take the day one step at a time.

Clara starts by walking over to the far side of the wardrobe and begins pushing it back into place. It doesn't move right away, feeling heavier than she remembers. She repositions, setting her back against the wardrobe and pushing hard with her legs. It must have been caught on something, because once it starts moving it slides quickly back into place, and Clara falls backward, landing on her butt beside it.

After a short rest, she gets dressed, pulling on one of the morning outfits her sister packed for her. The sound of her mothers' soft voices drifts to her ears from just beyond the door.

They speak in hushed tones, quiet enough she cannot make out what her mothers are discussing, but she doesn't have to hear to know it is most definitely about her.

Clara reminds herself the Passionflower dance last night wasn't a dream. At least that, she can hold onto.

Clara takes a deep breath before opening her door and stepping into the shared room. The room goes quiet.

Clara strides through the silence to the teapot waiting patiently in the small kitchenette. Unceremoniously, she selects a cup from the cabinet. Clara pours herself some tea, watching the rich brown swirl in the cup with satisfaction before either of her mother's speak.

"Good morning!" Aerin says cheerily followed by some muffled whispers.

Iris clears her throat.

"How'd you sleep, sweetie?" she asks.

"Fine," Clara replies shortly, sipping her tea and waiting for one of her mothers to ask their real question.

In truth, she didn't really know. The empty feeling in her chest and the heaviness in her limbs made her feel like she had slept only a few hours. She didn't remember when she had drifted off or even which memories from last night were real.

When Clara turns to place a hip against the counter, both of her mothers look as if they are holding their breath. She sighs.

"Out with it," she says, lifting the cup to her mouth.

"Well," Iris starts. "We just wanted to check in and, you know, see where your head's at."

"Because you know," Aerin starts, "you had been so upset when you found out you were picked for the Passionflower Ceremony, and–"

"I know," Clara interrupts, looking down at her tea as she stirs it, the small silver spoon clinking against the inside of the cup. "I didn't want to admit I loved him."

The words come out in a whisper, more to herself than them.

"But you do?" Iris asks, failing to keep the excitement out of her voice.

Clara takes a breath before meeting her eyes.

She nods, a slight smile playing at the edges of her lips. She had been so afraid of admitting her feelings to herself, but now, even not knowing whether Amor had truly come to see her last night, not knowing how he feels, her heart feels lighter. No longer weighed down by bricks and chains of unspoken words and forsaken feelings.

Iris smiles at her daughter and stands, pulling Clara into a delighted hug.

"My tea, Mom," Clara warns, almost spilling it.

Aarin stands and rescues the teacup from Clara's hands, smiling and rolling her eyes.

Iris just clings to her daughter and whispers in her ear. "I'm so happy for you, my love."

Clara relaxes into her mother's embrace.

"Thank you, mom," she whispers back.

When Iris finally releases her, Aerin returns the teacup with a smile.

"I think we should sit and talk about a few things," she says.

"Yes," Iris agrees, sitting back down at the tea table and motioning for Clara to join them. "Do you think Amor will complete his Passionflower Dance tonight? And if so, will you bond right away or wait a while?"

"Yes, and when you bond, will you two live here in Floria or Celeste?" Aerin asks.

"I..." Clara hesitates, unsure how to make sense of the swirling feelings inside, "don't know. I should talk to him." Clara sets her teacup on the table and turns to leave, anxious to get the whole thing over with.

Before she can take a step toward the door, Aerin catches her wrist.

"Amor will be busy with preparations for tonight. You likely won't get much of a chance to talk to him today, sweetheart," she says.

Clara reluctantly returns to her tea, sinking into the open chair. She looks down at her cup as she tries to organize her thoughts.

"Didn't you two discuss any plans during the mileway dances?" Aarin asks.

Clara shakes her head.

"I'm sure Amor was just as surprised as you two when I finished the Passionflower Dance and honestly, so was I," she says, leaning forward and stirring her tea absently. "I don't know if he will complete his Passionflower Dance, I don't know if he'll want to bond with me, which is why I need to talk to him."

Clara looks to her mothers for help.

Aarin and Iris share a glance before turning back to Clara.

"I'm sure it'll all work out," Iris says. "You may not get a chance to talk to Amor today, but there's always tomorrow."

"And even if Amor does finish his Passionflower Dance tonight, you two don't have to bond right away. You can take some time to figure things out," Aarin adds, trying to be helpful.

"And if he doesn't?" Clara asks, looking back down at her tea.

Her mothers are quiet.

The door to the hallway bursts open and Stella skips into the room.

"Clara, you're up, Finally!" Stella says brightly, rushing over to her. "Check out my arm!" She presents her right forearm to Clara.

Her fingertips are the same shade of crimson as her own, but the solid red stops at Stella's palm. Thin red lines and speckles of crimson decorate her wrist and forearm in a pattern reminiscent of a fireworks show.

"Let me see yours!" Stella pulls on Clara's right hand.

"Woah!" she exclaims as Clara extends her arm and Stella traces her fingers lightly across the red streaks beginning at her elbow and branch the rest of the way up her arm. "Yours goes all the way up onto your face," Stella says. "Vira's only went to her shoulder."

"Vira?" Clara questions.

"Yeah," Stella says. "She lasted almost to the end of the dance. Dropped her flower just seconds before you placed yours in the pool."

"Did you see her today?" Clara asks. She may not be able to talk to Amor, but if Vira is still around, well at least she can get some answers.

"Yeah, I saw her heading into the hedge maze just a few minutes ago," Stella says, confusion on her face.

# 16

❦

# Vira Nightshade

Clara rushes out to the gardens, taking the path into the hedge maze. She follows the same path Amor had taken the morning they had raced and as she rounds the last corner to see the flash of Vira's red wings, she freezes.

Why hadn't she taken any time to organize her thoughts before coming out here? What is she going to say to her?

Hey Vira, I know we haven't really talked at all, but I had an experience last night that I really hope wasn't a dream but probably was, so I wanted to ask you some questions to corroborate what the maybe dream and maybe real Amor said to me. Also, do you know anything about secret passageways that are sometimes there and sometimes not?

Vira would probably think she's crazy. The nymph sits facing away from her on the bench, her red wings moving slowly open and shut as she looks down at something on her lap.

Still frozen in the doorway to the center of the hedge maze, Clara attempts to come up with a sane way to start this conversation.

Her attention moves to the bright red spirals wrapping around the nymph's arm and up to her shoulder.

If Amor and Vira were just friends, like dream Amor had said, why had she held onto the flower for so long?

Vira turned, sensing Clara's presence.

"Vira," Clara says, her voice coming out a higher pitch than she intended. She clears her throat. "I didn't mean to interrupt," she says, stepping back in an effort to retreat.

"It's alright, I can share the bench," Vira states, scooting to make room. "Congratulations, by the way."

Vira grins at Clara.

"Thank you..." Clara replies hesitantly, not knowing what else to say. She stays planted in place.

Vira motions to the empty spot on the bench beside her. Clara feels like running away, but it is too late for her to escape now. Besides, she still has questions she needs answered, even if she is unsure how to ask them without coming across completely insane.

Taking a steadying breath, Clara walks to the bench and sits. She wonders if Vira is upset that she didn't complete her Passionflower Dance. Maybe even jealous Clara had.

The second Clara sits, Vira turns her attention back to the crystal tablet on her lap. In her right hand is a golden stylus that leaves iridescent lines where it meets the tablet.

Vira doesn't seem too upset. Clara glances over at her as the nymph spends a few quiet moments writing on her tablet. It appears to be some sort of letter, but Clara tries not to intrude.

Clara instead studies the art installation in front of them. The sculpture is different from the one a few nights ago. It must have been switched out quite recently.

Instead of metal, this sculpture is made of stained glass and depicts a hand holding a Florian passionflower. The sunlight bouncing off of it reflects colored beams of light onto the leaves around them.

"I know you probably don't like me very much," Vira states matter-of-factly as she puts a period at the end of a sentence and turns to lock Clara in her gaze. "I was never too concerned with making a good impression on you before. But I think there might be a few things I should clear up."

Clara's heart is thunderous in her chest. She was not expecting Vira to be so direct, and her intensity is intimidating.

"I'm not in love with Amor and he was never in love with me," she states.

Clara again feels like she is moving in slow motion, her mind taking longer than should be necessary to work through the words. Vira remains silent giving her time.

"Then why?" she asks, looking pointedly at Vira's arm.

Vira stretches her arm in front of her, examining it. The swirly designs resemble calligraphy.

"Oh this, no. Amor just owed me this," she says. "It was the least he could do for me after leading me on for so many years." She makes a disapproving clicking noise with her tongue.

"It took embarrassingly long for me to realize he didn't feel for me the way I felt about him, but once I did, it was obvious he only ever felt that way about you." Vira locks eyes with her again.

Appearing satisfied she had Clara's full attention, she sat back and turned her eyes to the glass flower.

"I was furious at him for a while. I wouldn't speak to him, pretended I couldn't hear him when he tried to talk to me, but eventually, I realized it was silly to ignore a friend just because he was in love with someone else." Vira glances sideways at Clara. "Don't you agree?"

That felt a little pointed, and Clara couldn't help feeling guilty about throwing away Amor's letters.

"I don't understand. Why did you take part in all of this?" Clara asks, finally finding her voice again.

Vira sighs.

"I plan to study cultural faethropology. I've applied to five different schools with good faethropology departments, but the one I really want to get into is quite competitive. Part of the application process is an essay on the culture of your hometown," she says, lifting the tablet from her lap. "I asked Amor to host this shindig so I could write an essay about the experience of being a candidate in a Florian Pairing Ceremony without having to host one myself. It's a pretty well-known cultural tradition, at least amongst cultural faethropologists, and showing up to my entrance interviews with this," she lifts up her right arm letting the colored lights shine across the swirling designs, "will make me a shoo-in."

"So Amor hosted a pairing ceremony just because you asked him to?" Clara asks.

"Well, he was probably going to do it eventually," Vira says, shrugging a shoulder, "but I needed the Passionflower Dance to be yesterday. I have my admission interviews scheduled throughout the next week. Plus," she threw a side-long glance at Clara. "I figured it would get you here, and I was sick of him moping about waiting for you to respond to his letters."

Clara's mind reels, and she's unsure whether she should be offended or impressed.

Vira places her hand on Clara's knee.

"I am truly happy for you and Amor. He is a great guy and he really loves you."

"He does?" Clara can't keep the doubt out of her voice.

Vira narrows her eyes at her. "Has he still not told you?"

"Well..." Clara starts, still unsure if last night was a dream or not.

Vira's confessions line up with what Amor had maybe said last night, but that wasn't really proof, and disappearing passageways still seems a bit far-fetched. Vira shakes her head and makes that clicking noise with her tongue again.

"Men," she huffs. "Well, I'm sure you'll see for yourself tonight at his Passionflower Dance. I suppose that means you two haven't talked about whether or not you will be bonding right away, or what you'll do after."

"Are you *that* sure he'll complete his Passionflower Dance?" Clara asks, and Vira laughs.

"Yeah," she says, rolling her eyes. "I have no doubts."

The knot in Clara's stomach starts to unwind, but the fluttering of wing beats quickly takes its place.

"Amor wants to travel," Vira says, interrupting Clara's excitement.

"I know," she says almost automatically. "I mean, he said he did the night of the Welcome Dance."

"And you?" Vira asks, her eyes probing.

"Me?"

Vira sighs. "Do you want to travel?" she clarifies.

Clara thinks about it. Traveling with Amor around the realm. It sounds heavenly. But what about her presentation, her plans for a garden in Celeste? If they're approved, she would need to be in Celeste for at least a decade, building and getting the plants rooted.

"Don't tie him down," Vira says. Clara looks up to meet her eyes. "He'll let you do it, but please don't," she turns her gaze away. "He's dreamed of traveling the realm for decades. He hasn't because he felt his mom needed him. If you two bond and you won't travel with him, he'll give it up."

Vira turns to her and grabs her hand.

"As his best friend, all I ask, is you make sure he travels. Even if that means waiting for the bond."

Vira's eyes hold Clara's, waiting. Clara nods, but Vira's gaze only intensifies.

"Promise me," she demands.

Clara clears her throat.

"I promise," she hears herself say, and as the words leave her lips, she feels the spoken contract snap into place. It's a strange sensation. Like a cord pulled tight and then plucked inside of her chest.

"Good," Vira says, tucking her tablet under her arm and standing.

"I'll hold you to it," she adds with a satisfied smile.

Clara recognizes something in Vira that reminds her of Jan. The fierce protection she has for Amor and his dreams, just like Jan has for her. Clara starts to wonder what Jan would think of all of this. Would she be just as concerned about Clara giving up her dream for Amor? She'd probably slap Clara for making a promise to Vira if she was here. That definitely could have been a mistake.

"Sorry I can't stick around for the rest of the festivities, but I've got lots of interviews to get in before this thing starts to fade," Vira says motioning to the designs. "I'm really glad I got a chance to speak to you before I left. I hope someday we can be friends." Vira waves, and with that she is gone.

Vira's blonde hair disappears behind a hedge wall as Clara sits stunned, turning everything that has happened this morning over in her mind.

*"Look at you, you're practically skipping," Jan says as they leave the library.*

"Shut up, I'm just excited," Clara scolds gently, shoving Jan's shoulder.

Jan slides out of the shove and turns to face her. She walks backward to stay a few feet in front of Clara as they head to their indoor horticulture class.

"It's been nine years since I've seen Amor and by this time tomorrow, I'll be there," Clara says.

"Are you going to tell him?" Jan asks, still walking backward.

"Tell him what?" Clara questions narrowing her eyes.

"That you looovvveee him," Jan says with a sly grin.

Clara rolls her eyes, but her uncontrollable smile is a dead giveaway. Clara sighs.

"I don't know," she says. "I mean, what if it messes up our friendship?"

"Girl, it's obvious he feels the same," Jan says, and when Clara looks questioningly at her, she adds, "Don't forget, I've read all of his letters too. Trust me, I'm usually right about these things."

With those words, Jan turns to walk forward, adjusting the book bag on her shoulders.

"Fine," Clara says. "I'll tell him."

"I'll hold you to that," Jan shoots over her shoulder.

**17**

❧

# His Passionflower Dance

Clara is entranced by the beauty of the ceremonial grounds. Though she's sure it looks much the same as it had the previous night, she had not taken the time to truly appreciate it then.

The candles lining the walkways and encircling the center circle emit a warm, calming glow that skips along the gilded pave stones. The silvery moonlight, cool and soothing, shines down, blanketing the park and melting into the dome of golden candlelight.

The pool in the center of the paved circle still contains the passionflower Clara placed in it the night before. Its tendrils move in slow, wavelike motions as it floats on the surface of the shimmering water.

Four of the five pedestals that surrounded the center pool the night before have been removed leaving only one. Atop it sits a small bowl of water and another Florian Passionflower, its fiery red petals splayed wide and purple tendrils hanging down from its perch above the water.

Clara looks up at the moon, brighter and bigger than the night before but not yet completely full. A sliver of shadow still lies across one side. Tomorrow that sliver of shadow would be gone and the moon would shine in its full brightness.

Clara had always loved being in Floria for the full moon. A few visits, after their mothers had tucked them in and returned to the full moon dance in the ballroom, she and Amor had snuck out to their fortress. They talked for hours as they lay watching the moonlight shine through the leaves.

The thought makes her heart flutter. She hadn't dreamed of this outcome, but it feels like a dream now. Perhaps everything, since she touched that flower, to this very moment, has been a dream.

Stella nudges Clara with her elbow, drawing her attention away from the moon and back down to earth. Clara turns her head to meet her sister's knowing gaze.

Stella smiles at Clara, giving her a moment to fully return to her body, then, with a quick tilting of her head, directs Clara's attention to the circle.

Across from Clara, the crowd splits open to allow Amor entrance to the circle. He steps forward onto the gilded stones, and Clara stops breathing.

As he makes his way to the pedestal his eyes search for hers.

Though all morning she had tried to find proof that Amor's visit the night before was more than just a dream, she had failed to convince herself. Now, as his eyes finally find hers, his smile is all the proof she needs. It was real.

Clara breathes a sigh of relief and smiles back, her heart nearly flying out of her chest.

Amor steps up to the pedestal and contemplates the passionflower. A hint of nervousness plays across his expression.

Amor absentmindedly rubs the side seam of his red silken pants between his fingers and thumb. He clenches both hands into fists at his sides, then releases them to adjust the white sash that lay across his chest. His gaze meets hers again as Madame Rose enters the circle.

"Welcome back everyone! We have made it to the final night of Amor Aiday's Pairing Ceremony. Tonight, Amor will attempt to complete the Passionflower Dance for Miss Clara Glade, who last night completed the Passionflower Dance for him."

She points to Clara and all eyes turn, causing her face to heat. Chewing on the inside of her lip, she smiles and waves. The eyes turn back to the center of the circle as Madame Rose continues.

"Clara proved to us last night that love can overcome pain. Now it is time for Amor to prove that love can overcome fear as well," Madame Rose says with a smile and a flourish. "It has been quite some time since we have had a Bonding Ceremony here in Floria, but if I were to make a prediction, I would say we will be having one again very soon."

Madame Rose hesitates for a moment, scanning the crowd with a grin.

"As early as tomorrow night, perhaps?" she adds with a wink.

The crowd cheers.

Clara turns to see Amor's reaction to the not-so-subtle suggestion and finds him smiling at her, a hint of a challenge in his eyes. The same expression he had when he asked her if she thought they could build a sky net in the woods.

Clara's stomach flutters. Would he really want to bond that soon? The thought that he might fills her with excitement.

She takes a deep breath to calm the rush of jitters. Amor turns to look at Madame Rose, waiting for his cue to start the dance.

Since they are no longer being held by Amor's gaze, Clara's eyes are free to wander down his face to his lips. She can still feel their touch from the previous night. The burning desire to press her lips against his again fills her.

Madame Rose joins the crowd, flicks her wrist as she had the night before, and the music begins.

Amor reaches down and lifts the flower with his left hand, starting his dance. Clara searches his face for signs of pain but sees none.

As Amor takes the first steps of the dance, Clara's eyes wander further down his body, drifting across his broad shoulders and down to his chest, which is only slightly covered by the white sash.

As he moves, the muscles in his chest and abdomen flex and relax. His leaf wings move in synchronization with his arm motions like a reflection.

He turns, and Clara traces her eyes across the veins of his wings as they stretch and bend. The muscles at their base contract and relax. Her eyes drop lower still, to his hips, and then wind their way back up his back to his shoulders, surveying every ripple of movement.

Clara's insides heat as she watches Amor dance. The sway of his hips, the strength in his legs as he lunges and steps gracefully around the pedestal. The shape of his arms and wings as he moves through the dance, turning and gliding across the golden pave stones.

Clara wonders if her dance the night before had filled Amor with the same desire she feels flowing through her body now. Clara's attention is drawn to his left arm by the redness starting to surface there, growing and spreading up toward his shoulder.

Clara peers back at Amor's face which looks still, frozen, determined. His eyes stare out into the empty space and she feels certain his mind is not really there in his body. Just as she experienced the night before, his mind was likely somewhere in their past.

The red streaks spread across his skin like brushstrokes, moving up his neck and down onto his chest, back, and rib cage. Clara brings her hand up to caress her own neck, remembering the burning sensations that left her skin dyed with the same red designs.

Amor finishes the last few steps of his dance and places the flower in the pool.

The moment his flower hits the water the tendrils reach out and wrap themselves around the tendrils of Clara's flower. It pulls itself to Clara's flower, drawing it close and interlacing their tendrils, causing both flowers to revolve around each other in the center of the pool.

Clara feels a jolt of energy run through her and reverberate along some new pathway between the two of them. For an instant, she can see Amor's hand in the water as if through his eyes. She feels a wave of completeness, joy, and ecstasy. Just as quickly as it emerged, the pathway fades and she is looking at Amor through her own eyes again.

It happened so swiftly that Clara is left wondering if she had imagined it.

Amor looks up from the pool and his eyes find hers instantly as if they were drawn by some magnetic force. A smile lights his face.

Clara, realizing she has been biting her lower lip, releases it to smile back at him.

The music stops and Marigold enters the circle, wrapping a silken sheet around Amor's shoulders and wings and leading him out of the circle. Clara can see from his dazed expression that his mind is swimming with memories and emotions, as hers had. She wonders what memories the passionflower venom might have shown him.

Clara steps away from the circle, squeezing through layers of guests so she can watch Amor as he and Marigold return to the main house.

A restlessness settles over her. She wants to run to him, to throw her arms around him, kiss him, but he probably needs time to collect himself.

Would he appear in her room again tonight? Now that she knew the passageway must be real, she hoped he would use it again. She simply couldn't wait till morning.

# Plums, Dreams, and Promises

Hours after the end of Amor's Passionflower Dance, Clara lies staring at the ceiling above her bed, waiting impatiently for a knock at her wardrobe. Once again, she runs through all of the questions she wants to ask Amor, if he ever shows up.

Questions like "What memories did the Passionflower venom show you?" and "How soon do you want to bond?" and "What's up with the disappearing passageway?" and "Do you maybe wanna kiss me again?"

If she was totally honest with herself, the last one might have to come first. The memory of Amor's kisses, the taste of his lips, and the urgency with which he held her had been driving her crazy.

Her stomach flutters with anxious energy. She closes her eyes, trying to calm herself, and immediately recalls the image of Amor's almost bare chest at the Passionflower Dance. She imagines herself tracing her fingers down from his neck over his bare skin and she can almost feel the heat of his body against her fingertips.

Clara's mouth waters at the thought. Swallowing hard, she sits up from her bed to pull herself back to the present.

The stillness is too much so she stands and paces quietly instead.

As she trails from the head of her bed to the wall on the other side of the room, something red catches her attention in her periphery. She turns to meet her reflection in the standing mirror.

Clara raises her scarlet hand and surveys it. For some reason, it just didn't feel like hers. Every time she'd seen her arm or her her face that day she was dazed for a moment. Like when she first cut her hair short and for a few weeks was surprised every time she saw her reflection.

Clara runs the fingers of her other hand lightly over the red skin. It's not painful or sore, the only time it ever really hurt was when the venom was in contact with her skin.

She continues running the fingers of her other hand from her wrist to her elbow where the solid red begins to separate into thick streaks that continue up to her shoulder. Clara traces a few of them with her fingers, stepping closer to the mirror as she continues following the new branching streaks with her eyes and fingers onto her chest.

Clara moves her hair off her shoulder and takes another step toward the mirror, turning her head slightly to follow a line climbing from her clavicle, up the side of her neck where it disappears behind her ear. She touches her face tracing one of the lines with her finger as it swirls and winds its way onto her temple.

Clara's seen similar designs dancing across the skin of other nymphs before. One of her visits when she was young took place shortly after an older nymph woman had bonded and her designs had not yet begun to fade. Seeing these designs on her own face feels surreal. Like a dream long forgotten.

She drops her hands to her sides and straightens her posture, meeting her reflected gaze and attempting to get used to the way she looks with the red designs dancing across the side of her face. Had they gotten longer since last night?

Her gaze drops to her chest where the streaks disappear under her nightgown, then further to the hem of her nightgown where the red swirls on her right thigh reach down toward her knee. She lightly brushes her fingers over her rib cage remembering the intense burning she had felt there.

Reaching down, she lifts the hem of her nightgown revealing more of the branching red lines. Still exploring the paths left by the passionflower venom, Clara pulls the nightgown over her head, letting it drop to the ground so she can examine the full design.

Turning to get a clear view of her reflection in the mirror, she sees the design resembles a tree. The thick trunk lay dense and scarlet against her rib cage all the way down to her hip where the roots diverge and twist along her curves and onto her thigh. From just under her breast the branching begins working its way up and along her chest, down her arm, and up into her neck and head.

It's beautiful.

She's beautiful.

Clara is still examining herself in the mirror, gently tracing branches and root lines with her fingers when a gentle knock disrupts her attention.

"Clara? Are you awake?" Amor whispers from the other side of the wardrobe.

Clara gasps, spinning around and instinctively moving her arms in front of her body before realizing Amor cannot see her with the wardrobe in the way. A thought plays in the back of her head, that maybe she would like him to, and she smiles at herself, shaking her head. Not the time.

"Yeah," she whispers back, picking up the nightgown and slipping it back on. "I'm awake, one sec."

Clara quietly pushes the wardrobe aside and before she can turn back to smile at him he takes her hand, interlacing his fingers in hers.

"Come with me," Amor says, pulling her through the passageway that has somehow reappeared behind the wardrobe.

Clara giggles, exhilaration flowing through her, and it feels like they're little again, sneaking out of the main house in the cover of the night.

The passageway is dark and cool with narrow stone walls that smell of petrichor. If Clara wasn't grounded by Amor's hand in hers she may have felt claustrophobic, but his touch eases any feelings of confinement.

When they exit the passageway Amor releases her hand, and Clara looks around to find they are in the main kitchen.

She hasn't been here since she was in her forties when she and Amor had snuck down here for a midnight snack.

That passageway would have been useful back then.

Clara suddenly remembers one of the questions she meant to ask and turns to see Amor swiping a few plums from the pantry.

"Hungry?" he asks with a smile that erases any other thought.

Clara nods, smiling back at him.

"These still your favorite?" he asks, tossing her one of the plums and tucking a bottle of white wine under his arm.

"Yeah," Clara says, "I haven't had one in a while though."

Amor opens the door leading outside, turning to offer his free hand to Clara.

"That's a shame," he says. "No plum trees in Celeste?"

Clara takes Amor's hand and he guides her out into the warm night air.

"No trees period," Clara says, taking a bite.

The plum is extra juicy and the juice drips down from her mouth and onto her chin. The drop rolls off her chin landing on her chest.

Amor laughs, pulling a small piece of fabric out of his pocket and wiping Clara's chin.

"Here," he says, handing the cloth to her.

He smiles and bites into his own plum as Clara takes the piece of fabric and finishes wiping her mouth, tapping where the drop had fallen on her chest before handing it back to Amor.

"Thanks," she says, pursing her lips and feeling a little embarrassed.

"Shall we?" he says, taking a few backward steps toward the forest while biting into his plum.

Clara takes a moment to really look at him for the first time since his dance.

He is wearing light, white linen pants and a matching long-sleeve shirt with the sleeves rolled up to his elbows. The neckline of the shirt is almost straight across except for a two-inch V in the center. A couple of thin red streaks can be seen through the V as he moves. His left hand and forearm are a solid scarlet color just like Clara's right. Clara can't help but wonder what the rest of his design looks like under his shirt.

Amor brings his plum to his lips with his scarlet hand, the wine bottle still clutched under his other arm. He looks expectantly at Clara.

Clara nods and steps forward, following him to the woods.

"So how'd I do?" Amor asks.

"Huh?" Clara responds.

"With the passionflower dance, did it look okay?" he clarifies.

"Oh, yeah, you looked really great. I mean, you did really great," she corrects, her ears feeling hot.

"Good, I was pretty nervous," he chuckles.

"Me too," Clara replies "You know, when I did mine."

"Well, you looked great too. I mean, did great."

He gives her a cheeky grin before taking another bite of his plum. Clara watches as the juice runs down his chin dripping onto his shirt and laughs, her nervousness dissolving like honey in water.

"Oops," he says, shrugging and laughing with her as he dabs his shirt with the cloth.

"So," Clara starts, swallowing another bite of her plum. "Binding Ceremony. Are you ready for that?" She takes her last bite and tosses the pit off into the forest.

"Are you asking if I know my steps or if I'm ready to be bound to you?" he counters.

Clara rolls her eyes. "Both I guess."

Amor tosses his plum pit to the side and takes her hand. Their skin sticks together from the remnants of the plum juice, but Clara doesn't mind.

"I'm ready," Amor says confidently, squeezing her hand for a heartbeat. "What about you?"

"I think I remember the steps," Clara replies with a sly grin as they near the rope ladder to their fortress.

Amor chuckles, stopping and pulling Clara's hand so she turns to face him. He captures her eyes with his.

"Are you ready to be bound to me, Clara?" he asks, a seriousness returning to his tone. "Because we can wait as long as you..."

"Yes," Clara interrupts. "I'm ready."

Amor leans forward placing his fingers under Clara's chin and kisses her deeply. His lips still taste like plums.

Clara's mind goes silent, lost in the tenderness of his touch.

"Hold this," Amor says, swinging the bottle of wine out from under his arm and pressing it into Clara's hands.

Turning, Amor climbs up the rope net ladder to the fortress, peeking his head over when he reaches the top.

"Okay, toss it," he says.

Clara laughs and tosses the bottle up to meet his hands.

"Why not just fly up, I mean you have wings that work just fine. I've seen it," Clara teases, climbing up the ladder herself.

"I don't know," Amor says, contemplating Clara's question. "I guess I feel like it's disrespectful to the fortress to not enter it as intended, ya know?"

Amor reaches down as Clara nears the top of the ladder to offer a steadying hand as she pulls herself the rest of the way.

"I mean, we built it when we both couldn't fly and the rope net ladder was the intended way up. Is that stupid?"

"No," Clara giggles. "It's kinda cute."

The smile Amor gives her in response is one she's seen many times on a much younger face. Warmth blooms in her chest at the sight. Seeing that expression again feels like a hug.

Amor takes a seat in the middle of the fortress floor, motioning for Clara to join him.

"I have a question," Clara states, joining him cross-legged in the middle of their fortress.

"I might have an answer," Amor replies with a smirk, uncorking the bottle of wine.

Clara rolls her eyes but can't help smiling.

"What did you see?" Clara asks.

A grin grows across Amor's face.

"I do have an answer," he says, nodding and then taking a swig of the wine.

"It's a little weird," he adds, offering Clara the bottle.

Clara takes the bottle from him.

"And?" she says, taking a swig herself.

Amor huffs a sigh.

"Well, we were, like, old," he starts. Clara almost spits out the wine in surprise.

"You mean it wasn't a memory?" Clara interrupts.

"You saw a memory?" Amor asks. "What memory?"

"No no, it's your turn," she says waving her hands in front of her. "Sorry, I interrupted, continue."

Amor narrows his eyes at her as she hands the bottle back to him.

"Fine, but that means it's your turn next," he warns. "Like I said, we were old and we were in a skyship that was parked right there." He points to a spot next to the edge of the fortress. "It was like a house on the inside. With a kitchen and a bedroom."

"Ok, so it's definitely not the actual future," Clara teases with a sly grin.

"Do you wanna go?" Amor asks with a laugh.

"I'm sorry, I'm sorry," Clara giggles, making the motion of sealing her lips.

"It..." he pauses, looking up as he recalls the visions, "It was more like a dream. We were in this skyship because it was our home, and we were cooking my mother's famous lentil soup together."

Clara can't help but laugh.

"So you dreamed of us making soup in a skyship tree house?"

"Are you making fun of my vision?" Amor asks sternly, putting his hand on his chest in fake offense.

Clara hesitates for a moment, weighing her response before nodding and saying.

"Yeah. That's exactly what I'm doing."

Amor roars with laughter, his posture relaxing as he rolls his eyes taking another sip of the wine. His smile is blinding.

"Your turn then?" he says after swallowing.

Clara narrows her eyes.

"That can't be it," she says, and the flush of pink on Amor's cheeks confirms it. "What are you not telling me?"

"Well," Amor says "I guess there's no point in being shy about it, given we'll be bound soon."

Despite his confident words, Amor hesitates, taking another sip from the bottle. Clara wonders if it's purely to add to the suspense or if he is truly nervous to say whatever is coming next.

"Well, we were kissing a lot while we cooked and when we finished adding all of the ingredients," Amor looks up, breaking their eye contact before saying, "Well, I did mention that the skyship also had a bedroom."

There are a few beats of silence before Amor looks back to see her very intrigued expression.

"And?" Clara asks, feigning ignorance and doing her best to quiet the squealing in her head. "What happened in the bedroom?" She suddenly feels quite hot and her heart is beating fast.

Amor rolls his eyes and inhales an uncontrollable smile on his face.

"I think you already have a pretty good idea," he says.

"What if I wanna hear you say it?" she challenges him, leaning forward and biting her lower lip. Her heart beats faster, and she wonders when she got so brave.

Amor lets out a resigned sigh looking down at his lap and then back at Clara.

"We made love," he says, his cheeks tinting a deeper shade of pink.

Clara screams internally and can't help but let a little squeak escape. She clamps her hand over her mouth to try to keep the rest in.

"Well, it sounds like your vision was a bit more entertaining than mine," she says once she has gotten herself under control.

"And that's a perfect segue, to your turn," Amor states handing her the wine bottle. "You saw a memory?"

Clara nods, taking a sip of wine. Maybe the sip he had taken wasn't just for suspense. The liquid seeps into her body and soothes the knot forming in her stomach.

"Must be a good one if it got you from calling me an asshole to confessing you love me," Amor teases.

Clara blushes at the thought of their brief yelling match.

"To be fair, this whole week has been bringing back buried memories. As for the one I saw in my Passionflower Dance, I wouldn't say the memory was a 'good' one, at least, not initially."

Amor's expression, a mix of concern and curiosity spurs her on.

Clara sighs. "Well, remember when I fell out of that tree?" Clara points at the tree behind her and Amor nods. "In the memory, I was standing down on the ground and watched the whole thing happen. I saw you run to me. You seemed so scared."

"I was," Amor says, his eyes distant, his expression serious again, and his face almost white.

"And then you grabbed the sled we used for the ropes and lifted me onto it. I followed the young you as you pulled me to the main house. Then everything went dark for a bit and we were in the med bay late that night. You were still there, passed out in a chair, and obviously hadn't left since you had gotten me there."

Amor half smiles. "My mom had tried to get me back to the room to change, but I refused to let you out of my sight."

Clara reaches across the short distance between them to grab his hand.

"I heard myself whisper your name and I turned to see the younger me just waking up in the med bay bed," she continues. "And I could see the love in her eyes as she looked at you. As I looked at you sleeping in that chair."

Clara looks down at their hands as Amor gently traces his thumb back and forth over her palm.

"I feel like I locked that little girl away in my memory after the last time I was here. Forgot about her and her love, her hopes, and dreams."

Clara clears her throat, meeting Amor's gaze.

"I'm not sure why I got near-death experience memories while you got sex dreams in a skyship-treehouse," Clara smiles as Amor's mouth drops open at her directness.

He huffs a laugh and runs his hand through his hair, the blood flowing back into his face. Shaking his head and pressing his tongue against the bottom of his teeth, he turns back to her.

Amor searches her eyes for a breath, his broad smile softening into a pensive expression.

"Maybe you needed to remember that part of you before you could accept her dreams. I had already accepted my love for you, so it showed me my dreams for our future," Amor suggests.

"Which is to live in a skyship-treehouse? And make soup?" Clara asks, lifting an eyebrow and smirking at him. She is not going to let him forget that part. Amor fights another laugh but can't keep from smiling.

"I don't care where we live," he says, shaking his head and taking her other hand more fully. "I just want to be together. You and I, for all the centuries to come."

"I want that too," Clara says, beaming. Amor leans forward, gently pulling her hand toward him. She shifts onto her knees to better close the distance between them and presses her lips to his.

His free hand finds its way to the side of her neck, gliding up and back till his fingers are intertwined with her hair. Amor deepens the kiss, pulling her into him and Clara melts onto his lap.

When they finally separate for air, Amor whispers, "Will you bond with me tomorrow?"

Clara's internal ecstasy is cut short as she feels that sensation in her chest like a cord being plucked. Her promise to Vira drifts through her mind. She scoots away from him, sitting back down on the netting floor in front of him.

When she looks up to meet his confused eyes she sighs.

"I don't think I can travel with you," she says. "Maybe we should wait until after your trip to bond."

Amor looks stunned.

"You wouldn't want to come with me?"

"It's not about what I want, it's..." Clara hesitates trying to organize her thoughts into words. "I told you about the proposal I'm making to the Celeste City Council when I get home."

"The garden?" Amor says, nodding.

"Yes, well if they accept the proposal, I'll be under contract. I'll have to be in Celeste for at least a decade to get the structures built and get the plants big enough to not need daily care," Clara explains.

Amor is quiet for a while.

"Well, that's okay," he finally says. "What's a decade when we have centuries? I can wait to travel."

Amor reaches for her hands, but she pulls them away.

"Amor, I won't tie you down. How long have you dreamt of traveling the realm?" she asks, already knowing the answer.

He doesn't respond, just turns his gaze away from her, a crease forming between his brows.

"How long have you already waited?" she asks.

"I've waited for you longer," he whispers, meeting her gaze again. "I could wait another century if it meant you could come with me."

Clara shakes her head adamantly. "I can't let you do that."

"Why not?" Amor asks.

It's Clara's turn to look away in silence.

"Is it not my decision?" Amor asks, turning her face back toward him. His hold on her face is firm, unwavering, and the confusion in his eyes makes her heart ache. "I don't want to spend another second separated by an ocean. Do you?" His eyes search hers for an answer.

"Of course not, but," Clara says, pulling her face from his grip, "I've made a promise."

Surprise flashes across his face and he drops his hand.

"My mother?"

Clara shakes her head huffing a laugh. "Vira, actually."

"By the river, Clara, why would you do that?" Amor grumbles, standing up and turning away from her. "What exactly did you promise?"

He starts to pace across the netting, each step causes Clara to bounce slightly.

Clara heaves a sigh.

"That I make sure you travel, even if it means we wait for the bond."

"Aha," he says with a smile. "She didn't say when I would have to travel, just that you make sure I do, and I will, eventually."

"You sound like an old elf searching for loopholes," Clara says, shaking her head.

The comment earns her a dirty look from Amor.

"Well, I wouldn't have to search for a loophole if you hadn't made a promise," he snaps.

Clara is taken aback by the level of rage and accusation in his words.

"You should know better than to make promises."

"What about when you promised yourself to never bond with anyone?" Clara says defensively.

Amor stops pacing and his hands ball into fists.

"Exactly my point, you have no idea what I had to go through to release myself from that promise," he says through clenched teeth.

Clara has never really understood why fae felt obligated to keep promises to themselves. As both the promisor and promisee, could he not just release himself from the bond?

Amor stares up at the leaves, his fists still clenched. Clara starts to open her mouth to ask for clarification, but Amor speaks again.

"It's getting late. We can talk about this more tomorrow." Without waiting for a response, he spreads his wings and flies down to the forest floor.

# 19

# Don't Chicken Out

Clara is out of her room the second the candles spark to life. It is officially "tomorrow" and she is going to have this conversation before the fear and dread can immobilize her.

She has been trying to plan out her words for hours, but that never seems to work anyway. She's done thinking, she just needs to speak and whatever comes out, comes out.

She climbs the stairs and goes over the main points she wants to make:

First, Amor was right, she didn't want to spend any more time separated by an ocean.

Second, she did know better than to make a promise, but she had because she agreed with Vira. Amor's dreams are worth protecting and Clara would hate herself if she became the thing keeping him chained in one place.

Thirdly, she knew Amor always put his loved ones before himself and unless Clara put him first, his dreams would always come last.

She reaches the top of the stairs and turns down the first hallway. It was not part of her plan, but traveling around the realm with Amor really does sound blissful. For that, she could postpone her proposal. She may even be able to improve her designs between now and then.

She wanted to bond tonight and she would keep her promise to Vira without the need of a loophole.

She rounds the corner and takes the last few steps to his door. The words hit her ears like a kick to the face and she freezes a step away from the door.

"I'm not ready." Amor's tone sounds so final and her heart drops to the cold floor. "I know I told her I was, but It was a lie. I'm not ready."

Clara's heart stops. Did he change his mind? Does he want to wait now? It had been her suggestion to do so last night, but she had since gotten used to the idea of bonding with Amor tonight under the full moon. Of traveling the realm with him in newly bonded bliss.

It is a new dream and she isn't done mourning her old one, but to her surprise, this new one feels even harder to let go of.

"It seemed perfect, but now it just feels off. " Amor says.

"Chill bro," came Tommy's voice, "are you sure you're not just overthinking it?"

Clara unconsciously holds her breath.

"No, I'm sure," Amor confirms. The next few syllables are drowned out by the scrapping of wood against stone. "-just doesn't feel the way I wanted it to. There's something missing."

Clara exhales slowly. Unsteadily. She takes a couple of steps away from the door. Her heart starts beating faster, and the hallway feels like it's shrinking.

"Well, what's missing?" Tommy asks.

There's silence for a few seconds.

"Love?" Amor says, sounding unsure. "It should be there, mixed in with all the other emotions, but it's just not."

Clara turns away from the door. Her vision goes blurry. Did he not love her? Though she no longer wanted to, she could bear waiting to bond till he finished his travels, but if he didn't feel love for her, did that mean they would never bond?

She steps away from the door.


*There was a knock on the door to the shared room in their usual suite in the Floria main house. Aerin got up from her seat by the window and walked over to open it.*

*"Thank you," she said to the fae on the other side before closing the door. "Clara, you have a letter."*

*Clara looked up from her coffee surprised and confused. She had never gotten a letter while she was in Floria before. Aerin handed it to her and she immediately recognized the handwriting from the notes Jan would always slip her in class.*

*She ripped it open and scrawled on the paper inside were the words. "Don't Chicken Out, XOXO -Jan" Clara rolled her eyes and laughed, but the smile didn't last long.*

*It felt like Amor had been avoiding her the whole trip and after what she overheard at the bonfire and the kiss she saw between Amor and that girl, she was certain Jan was wrong about Amor loving her.*

*Clara wondered if Jan would admit she was wrong when Clara told her all that had happened. She could write her back, but she'd already be on the skyship home by the time the message got to her. She might as well wait till she could tell her in person. Clara wondered if she would still think her a chicken for not telling him after everything.*

*"I'm gonna go for a walk," Clara said, excusing herself from the room and heading out to the garden.*

*Turning into the hedge maze, Clara made her way to the center deep in thought.*

*She stared down at the letter, focused on those three words until she turned a corner and ran into a body.*

*"Pardon me," she said, looking up to see Amor, his face just lifting from the book he was reading.*

*"Clara," he said, as surprised as her.*

*"Amor," she said barely a whisper.*

*Quiet followed, and Amor looked away, breaking eye contact.*

*"You're leaving today, aren't you?" he asked, looking up and then down at his feet. Anywhere but at her.*

*"Yeah," she said, clutching the letter behind her back. "The skyship should be here to pick us up in a few hours.*

*More quiet as Amor nodded, looking somewhat sad.*

*I love you. Clara said the words in her head, but she couldn't open her mouth. She clutched the paper more tightly behind her back.*

*Amor's eyes met hers and he opened his mouth. He looked as if he wanted to say something important, but he hesitated. The look in his eyes made Clara think, despite everything, the words she could not get herself to utter might just leave his lips.*

*But they didn't, and she didn't say it either.*

Clara lifts her back foot off the ground to take another step away from Amor's door but puts it back down.

She is not letting herself run this time. She came here to talk, and she is going to be heard.

Turning on her heels and stepping back up to the door, Clara knocks before she can change her mind. The voices on the other side of the door continue, but Clara can also hear footsteps.

"Well it sounds like you've made your decision," Tommy says.

The door handle turns and the door starts swinging open.

"You just have to tell her," Tommy says.

As Amor pulls the door open the rest of the way, he turns from Tommy and finds Clara standing in the doorway. His mouth opens to say something, but Clara beats him to it.

"I love you," She says the second his eyes reach her, her tone more intense than she had meant it to be. A few seconds of silence pass as Amor's eyes scan her face. The tilt of his brow makes him appear confused by her declaration.

"I love you too," he says slowly.

More silence follows as they both look at each other. Clara didn't know where to go from here, and Amor's confusion only compounded her own.

Tommy clears his throat.

"I should let you two chat," he says, stepping toward the door.

"Um," he adds, looking between Amor and Clara, both frozen on opposite sides of the doorway.

When neither of them moves he ducks under Amor's arm and shimmies through the doorway, his back against the door frame in an effort to slip past them.

"Talk more later?" he says to Amor as he backsteps away, but Amor's eyes are still locked on Clara.

Tommy doesn't wait for a response and disappears down the hall.

"Do you want to come in?" Amor finally says, stepping back and motioning for her to enter the room.

Clara nods and steps into the room. Amor lets the door close behind him, turning to face her.

"What's going on?" Amor asks.

"I was about to ask the same thing," Clara says.

"Well, I asked first," Amor says with a joking smile, narrowing his eyes.

Clara sighs. "I heard some of your conversation with Tommy," she admits.

"Oh?" Amor says looking even more confused.

Clara starts fiddling with her fingers and averts her gaze, pretending to look at some of the papers scattered across his desk.

"It's ok if you're not ready," she starts "I mean I suggested we wait to bond last night."

When he says nothing, Clara reluctantly looks up at his face she sees his brow furrowed in confusion. His eyes move from side to side as if trying to recall what all she could have overheard.

"Clara..." he starts but doesn't seem to know what to say.

"If you don't love me–" Clara continues, looking back down at the desk and picking at the edge of one of the papers.

"Hold up," Amor interrupts, stepping to her and capturing her hand.

She doesn't look at him, not wanting him to see the tears threatening to overflow from her eyes, but he gently grips her chin and turns her face to his.

"I love you, Clara," he says, this time the words are just as intense as they had been when she spoke.

It's Clara's turn to be confused and she furrows her brows, a tinge of anger growing in her chest.

"But–" she starts.

"I wasn't talking about not being ready to bond with you. I was talking about my book," he says.

He releases her chin and starts gathering the papers on his desk together.

"I was telling Tommy about how I told my publisher I would be ready to publish my second book before I went on my trip, but the climax just doesn't feel the way I want it to, it's missing something," he explains, turning back to her.

"Love?" Clara asks.

"Well, yeah," Amor shrugs and Clara starts laughing.

Amor wrinkles his brow again. "Why are you laughing?"

"I just–" Clara takes a few breaths to quell her laughter. "I guess I have a bad habit of overhearing things and jumping to the worst possible conclusion. I don't know why I find that so funny right now but..."

Amor smiles and steps toward her, wrapping his arms around her.

"I love you, Clara," he says again, "and I'm ready to bond with you whenever you want. Even if that's not tonight. Just please let me come back to Celeste with you."

Clara starts pushing away from Amor's embrace. This conversation started off on a completely different track than she had planned on her way up here. Clara decides to restart.

"I'm not going to let you give up on traveling, Amor."

"I'm not," he insists, pulling her back into his chest. "I'm traveling to Celeste. It was going to be my first stop anyway and I still haven't decided how long it will take to fully explore the city. I heard it's quite big," he says.

Clara looks up to see him grinning down at her.

"Compared to Floria, it's huge," she says, unable to hold back her smile, "but not a decade to explore huge."

"I had an idea about that," Amor says, releasing her and walking over to his bookshelf. He pulls out a book on horticulture.

"Are you planning on starting the garden plants from seed?" he asks as he flips through the pages.

"Yeah," Clara responds, curiosity budding in her chest.

"Well, what if you used cuttings for the slower-growing plants at least?" he says, finding his page and handing the open book to Clara.

She looked down to see a chapter on propagation. She exhales quickly.

"How did I not think of this?" she says, flipping through the chapter. "I propagate plants all the time at the farming tower, it would cut the growth time in half, at least, but..."

She hesitates and then an inspired grin spreads across her face.

"I might need to go to a few places to collect the cuttings."

Amor squints at her, tilting his head, and her smile widens.

"My garden design includes plants from all over the fae realm," Clara explains "There won't be anywhere to get live cuttings for most of them on the elven continent, but the time and labor saved from cutting the growth time could be allocated to a few intercontinental trips."

Amor smiles.

"See," he says, stepping close to her "I knew we could figure it out."

Clara laughs again.

She takes a deep breath thinking about how much easier it will be when they can communicate without words. When they are bonded and can feel each other's emotions and hear each other's thoughts.

"I want to bond with you tonight," she says, looking up at him again.

"As you wish, my lady," he says with a bow. "I'll have to let Madame Rose know."

"And I'll have to redo my project timeline," Clara laughs. "Oh, and the budget. I've got a lot of work to do before Beltane."

"Tomorrow though," Amor says, wrapping his arms around her. "We can go to the library and I'll write while you work."

"That sounds perfect," Clara says with a smile, burying her face in his chest.

# 20

# Binding Ceremony

"Knock knock," Aerin says cheerily, throwing the door open and gliding into the room with Iris and Stella trailing her.

"Oh my gods, Clara, you look beautiful!" Aerin gasps at the sight of her.

Clara smiles at her mother who is now starting to tear up.

"Thank you, Mom," she says, hugging her.

As soon as they separate, Iris rushes forward and takes Clara's hands looking into her eyes investigatively.

"Are you certain about this, Clara? I mean, it's no secret that I love the thought of you and Amor together, but I want to make sure this is something you really want to do because..."

Clara smiles at her mother and puts up her hand to silence her.

"I want this," she says. "I am very certain."

Her mother hugs her tight. "I'm so happy for you, baby," she whispers.

When Iris releases her, Clara reaches her hand out for her sister who obediently takes her hand and pulls herself in for a hug.

"I suspect you knew this was coming the moment we got those invitations," Clara whispers in her sister's ear.

Stella always had the impeccable ability to know how those around her felt, even when they didn't.

"I had a hunch," she replies with a smile.

Clara rolls her eyes as they step apart, then takes hold of her sister's hands. Music trickles in from outside as Clara squeezes Stella's hands with excitement.

"Are you ready?" Stella asks seriously but with a smile.

Clara takes a deep breath.

"Absolutely."

The sisters smile at each other. Stella lets go of Clara's hands and reaches for the door. Clara's mothers step to either side of her, interlacing their arms with hers.

Iris and Aerin escort Clara past a bubbly Stella, who graciously holds the door. Together, they stride out into the park, leading her slowly down the twisting path to the ceremonial circle. Lines of fae greet them excitedly, holding candles to light their path.

The moon above is at its peak fullness and looks larger and brighter than Clara has ever seen it. She can't help but feel like the stars have aligned specifically for this moment.

Across the park, another line of fae spirals off toward a different dressing room. Clara can't see Amor through the crowds, but she knows he and Marigold are making their way to the ceremonial circle as well.

Clara's heart flutters as she walks, and she grips tightly to her mothers' arms. As they proceed, the bustling crowd lining their path hurriedly falls in step behind.

Her pace is quicker than it probably should be, but she doesn't care. This path is the only thing standing between her and Amor, and it is simply too long.

When they finally reach the circle, the crowd of onlookers part to reveal Amor and Marigold on the opposite side of the paved circle.

Clara's heart swells when she sees him in the purple suit he had picked out that morning. He said he liked it because it matched the color of her wings. She had joked that she should wear green then, and he had smiled at her, pulling her close, and told her to wear the dress she had worn for their Mileway Dance.

Across the circle, Amor looks her up and down just like he had the night of the Mileway Dance, and beams at her. How had she not seen what he felt for her back then when it is so clear now?

Her mothers and Marigold stop at the edge of the pave stones, proudly releasing their hold on their children. Clara steps forward into the circle, eyes tied to Amor's and he does the same.

Clara and Amor take three quick, long, strides toward each other like two magnets drawn to touch. They take each other's hands and smile broadly.

Amor looks to his left, at the center pool that holds their passionflowers. They float along the surface together with their tendrils still intertwined. Amor lifts Clara's right hand and clasps it tightly in his.

"Ready to be stuck with me?" Amor asks with a smile.

"Beyond ready," Clara replies.

The music begins and they plunge their hands into the pool. The flowers' tendrils wrap around their clasped hands and music starts to play. The venom of the flowers burns and spreads. Clara grips Amor's hand tighter.

Amor places his free hand on Clara's waist and she places hers on the back of his shoulder pulling him into her and then lightly tracing a finger up the back of his neck.

Amor's eyes widen and he wraps his arms around her, bringing his hand to her lower back and pulling her closer against him. His touch grounds her, and she realizes that the burning venom feels less intense in his arms.

They lift their clasped hands out of the water, bringing the flowers with them as they begin to spin and glide around the circle. They hold each other close and let the venom from the passion flowers seep into them. Clara's vision begins to blur and images and emotions flash through her head, blending and merging together.

*Two babies cuddled together in a crib feeling warm and safe.*

*Toddlers crawling through the grass exploring a new world together and the accompanying wonder and curiosity.*

*A young boy and girl running through the hedge maze with excitement and pure joy.*

*Two kids climbed trees, reaching closer and closer to the sky. Their chests, full of exhilaration as they cling to the branches only a few feet off the ground.*

*The delight of receiving a letter in the mail and reading about all the things going on in their friend's life. Writing a letter back to answer all the questions within.*

*The anticipation of counting down the days, hours, minutes till they would next see each other.*

*The two of them playing in their Fortress, developing secret handshakes, feeling the warmth and support of each other's friendship.*

*As the images fly by, emotions fill her, and not just her emotions, but his too. She again watches herself fall from the tree, but instead of only seeing the look on Amor's face, this time she feels Amor's terror at the thought of losing his friend.*

*Clara sees herself awakening again in the medical wing, Amor slouched in the chair by the bed. Her heart feels again that first spark of love beyond friendship.*

*Amor's eyes flutter open to see Clara smiling at him and she feels the relief lift from his chest. He jumps from his chair and wraps his arms around her, tears streaming down his face, and it feels like their emotions mix and meld inside of her.*

*Amor looks up from the ground at Clara again climbing the tree she had fallen out of the day before, shaking his head. On the outside, he looked disapproving, but as Clara watches the scene before her, she can feel what he truly felt in that moment. Admiration, and the first spark of love beyond friendship. Amor grabbed a few ropes off the ground and began climbing up into the tree to join his friend.*

*The visions continue and she sees her and Amor grow bigger and taller. She sees parts of Amor's life that she wasn't there for, like the death of his father. She feels the despair he felt as tears ran down his face.*

*She sees the day of his father's funeral, and feels that plucking sensation in her chest when Amor promised himself to never love anyone the way his mother loved his father, and the promise snaped into place.*

*She feels the same plucking sensation when she sees the young Amor watching Clara and Stella as they practiced the passionflower dance in the ceremonial circle later that day. Feels his conflicting emotions bubble over into anger and then a twinge of regret as he walked away.*

*She sees the skyship land and herself run out, grabbing his hand and pulling him immediately toward the woods. Feels the return of his feeling for her up in the fortress. The way it cracked the stone walls he had built around his heart in the decade since they had last seen each other. She feels the same plucking sensation in her chest and his realization that his feelings for her had not changed. She feels his urge to flee.*

*She sees the evening on the shore of the river surrounded by bonfires and feels the internal battle warring beneath the surface. The consistent plucking sensation every time he looked over at her.*

*She feels the fear that rose in his chest when Tommy pointed out she had been looking at him too.*

*She sees the memory of his mother crumpled on the floor of her room sobbing flash though his mind as he said "Yeah, it's like she's in love with me or something."*

*She feels how his body had cleared of emotion when Vira kissed him. No plucking sensation in his chest, no fear.*

*She feels the despair and the tears as Amor sat in his room watching her skyship float into the sky through his window.*

*She sees Vira re-shelving books in the library.*

*"She still hasn't replied to any of your letters?" she asked.*

*"No, but to be fair, I haven't sent her one in quite a while." Clara feels every bit of guilt, regret, and longing in Amor's words.*

*"Well, I think I have a plan that could kill two birds with one stone. Repay your debt to me and possibly get her back to Floria," Vira said with a sly grin on her face.*

*"I'm listening," Amor replied with a spark of hope.*

*"Host a Pairing Ceremony."*

*"The Glade's RSVP'd," Marigold said, walking into the dining room.*

*"Clara?" came Amor's response, putting down his fork.*

*"Yes, and Stella and Iris and Aerin of course."*

*Clara can feel his excitement mixed with just a hint of fear.*

*She sees flashes of the last seven days, feeling Amor's emotions throughout.*

*She watches him look for her as he walked down the stairs on the night of the welcome dance. Feels the moment of inspiration when her mothers said she had just disappeared. Feels the all-consuming love he felt when he saw her again for the first time.*

*She sees the name dance and their race through the maze. She sees the Trivia Dance and Mileway Dance. All through his eyes.*

*She feels his hurt when she yelled at him and his confusion as she completed the Passionflower Dance. Feels His urgency and nervousness the night he came to see her and his pure joy when she told him she loved him.*

*A cool sensation runs through her, easing the burning flame she only senses now in its absence.*

Clara's vision clears and she and Amor lock eyes.

She can feel the same pathway between them that she felt after his Passionflower Dance, but this time it is solid and it doesn't fade.

"Hey, Amor?" Clara sends the words soundlessly down the pathway.

"Yeah?" she hears his voice in her head.

"I fell for you first," she says down their new bond, sending an image of the younger Amor looking up at her as she climbed the tree the day after she had fallen.

Amor laughs and rolls his eyes.

"It's always gotta be a competition with you," he sends back shaking his head and smiling. Along with the words comes a wave of love and joy.

Clara rises to her toes and kisses him. The wave grows, filling them both with pure ecstasy as the music fades and the crowd around them cheers.

# 21

# Beltane Council Meeting

Clara takes in the sight of the golden gates surrounding the Celeste palace. The gates reach high into the sky, completely enveloping the palace so as to protect it, not from intruders but from the sun and the sand of the surrounding desert.

Large metal panels sculpted to look like leaves and petals tessellate together to form the gate, held in place by thick wires that have been bent and molded to resemble vines. Where the walkway in front of them meets the gate, an extra large panel, shaped like the sun rising on the horizon has been turned, creating two large doorways on either side.

This is the latest masterpiece by Charles Daves, and as Clara stands outside admiring it, she thinks it may very well be her favorite.

Clara's stomach flutters as the realization sinks into her skin. Soon she will be pitching her garden designs to Daves and the rest of the council.

A light squeeze on one of her hands brings her back to the present and she looks to her left to meet Stella's gaze. Stella smiles at her warmly.

"You got this," she says.

Clara turns her head to the right to receive a comforting grin from Amor. Behind her, she can feel the presence of her mothers. It feels like a blanket of protection and calming support wrapped around her.

Clara is suddenly uncomfortably aware she has been standing in front of the open gate for quite some time now. She also recognizes that the rest of her group has been standing patiently, waiting for her.

She wouldn't say she feels ready for what comes next. Even so, she's pretty sure that staring at the gate any longer will not help her feel more ready, so she steps forward and everyone else follows.

They enter through the gate and continue forward toward the palace. The ancient sandstone structure radiates an energy much different from that of the gate.

Where the gate feels polished, refined, and innovative, the palace itself feels as though it was forged from the sands of time. From millennia.

Though it once housed Kings and Queens, the palace now serves as the home and offices of the Celeste Council members and their families.

The walls are made of stratified sandstone with varying shades of red, orange, and yellow. Colored Glass windows adorn the building casting kaleidoscopic light into the building. The entire palace was carved from what used to be a small mountain and charmed with Fae magic to hold up against weathering.

The palace is the oldest building in Celeste. Not because it was the first built but rather that all others built before it have since been knocked down to make way for newer construction, or altered and updated so much that they could not reasonably be considered the same building.

For the sake of preserving history, many mage hours have been dedicated to protecting and maintaining the palace and keeping its sandstone walls from weathering.

Clara and her entourage enter the throne room where the council hears disputes and proposals from the citizens of Celeste.

Along the walls on either side of her are seats for citizens who wish to observe. Several fae sit and chat in small groups, a few of them looking up to check out the new arrivals.

Directly in front of her, seven large stone seats sit empty, elevated at the top of a broad set of stairs.

Clara feels a hand slip from hers and turns to see Stella and her mothers moving to some empty seats on the side of the room. She turns to Amor, thankful for his grounding presence. Amor looks around the room before meeting Clara's eyes.

"Not as many people as I expected," Amor says. "I thought there were like thousands of fae here in Celeste?" he questions, a wrinkle forming between his brows.

Clara smiles at him. "Try tens of thousands, but not everyone goes to every council meeting here. It's not like in Floria. There wouldn't be a room large enough in Celeste for that," she says.

"It tends to just be the people who are scheduled to speak, like me and them," Clara says, pointing to a group of fae standing or pacing by the entrance flipping through papers and mouthing words to themselves.

"Their loved ones," she continues, motioning toward the small groups of people sitting in the seats to their left, "and the few fae who have some sort of personal interest in the topics being presented." She motions to a few fae sitting by themselves or in pairs throughout the seating area to their right.

"I see," Amor says. "And the only ones who can speak during the meeting are the people scheduled?" he confirms, and Clara nods.

"Weird," he says, shrugging and following Clara to meet up with Stella and their moms.

Almost as soon as they sit down a door opens and all chattering in the room stops. All eyes turn to the front of the room as the seven council members enter and take their seats at the top of the staircase. Clara recognizes the last to enter as Charles Daves.

He is the tallest among them and wears a pleated black suit with a shiny silver tie. There is not a single wrinkle on his suit or his face.

"Thank you all for coming!" says the elder woman, standing in front of the middle chair. Her long silver hair is braided down her back and almost touches the floor. "We are very eager to hear what you all have for us today."

"That's Elise Harthrone," Clara says through her bond with Amor. "She's the granddaughter of the last elven monarch, daughter of the first head of the council, and has been elected as head of the council for the last three terms."

Elise bows to the room before taking a seat. As she does, so do the rest of the council members.

A young fae with a scroll in her hands steps onto the lowest stair, turning to face the rest of the room. She looks down at the scroll.

"First we will hear from Aaron Skimmer who wishes to make a proposal for a public bathhouse," the young elf says.

A large fae with green scales on his face and the back of his hands stands. He has a determined look on his face and steps to the center of the floor.

"I'm sorry, I will give you a chance to speak, but if I'm not mistaken we had this same proposal made to the council in our Samhain meeting. Have you sufficiently changed your proposal since then or are you just wasting our time?" Charles Daves asks flatly, leaning back in his chair lazily.

"Umm," Mr. Skimmer stutters. "I have added a private bath area for those who don't feel comfortable bathing in public."

"Is that all?" Daves says unimpressed.

"Well..." Skimmer trails off.

"With all due respect, Mr. Skimmer, the lack of a private bath option was not the main issue the Council stated in our denial of your Samhain proposal. It was the use of water. Celeste is in the middle of the desert. Water is a precious resource and I'm sorry to say the benefit provided by a public bathhouse is not worth the amount of water that will be needed to maintain it. Unless you have made changes that either drastically reduce the project's water usage or found some new and plentiful water source, I'm going to have to ask you to sit down," Charles Daves states and Skimmer reluctantly sulks back to his seat.

"Fuck," Clara thinks.

"What?" Amor asks through their bond.

"That's what I was worried about. There are so many benefits to gardens, but part of the reason we don't have one yet is that it takes a fair bit of water to grow all the plants for it."

"Is there any way to have the plants harvest their own water?" Amor asks. He senses her confusion and continues, "I worked in the kitchen for a bit and the cooks keep an herb garden but don't really have time to tend it, so whenever there's a problem, like pests or depleted soil, they find and plant something that does the job for them. Like alliums to deter pests or beans to replenish the soil nutrients."

Clara contemplates for a moment.

"So I need a plant that can... what? Absorb water from the air? Collect and store water?"

Inspiration.

Digging into her bag and pulling out a pencil, Clara flips open her book of designs, sketching fiercely, no longer paying attention to what is happening on the floor until...

"Clara Glade," says the fae with the scroll. "With a presentation for a garden."

Clara hurriedly gathers together her papers, her fingers fumbling in her rush to stand up. Amor touches her hand as she rises and she meets his eyes.

"Breathe," he says, "You got this." His touch soothes her impatience. Breathing slowly, she allows herself the time she needs to refocus on her presentation.

"Thank you," she sends along the bond, taking another breath before stepping onto the floor.

As Clara looks up at the seven council members before her, Charles Daves leans forward in his chair. Elise Harthrone smiles at her encouragingly.

"I have here my blueprints, design sketches, project timeline, and budget," Clara says, stepping forward to hand the papers to the head of the council.

The Fae with the scroll steps toward her, hand out for the papers, and Clara feels a flush of embarrassment. Of course, she shouldn't be handing the papers directly to the head of the council.

She gives them to the fae with the scroll who distributes them to the council members.

Clara clears her throat and tries to get back on track.

"Plants have value beyond their ability to feed us. In addition to their ability to be used in medicines even," she says scanning the council. "Just being in the presence of plants can lower a fae's stress levels and improve their mood."

She glances at Charles as his eyes scan over her drawings and designs.

"I understand that we live in a desert and water is precious, and I will admit that my plans will require water to grow and maintain." Daves looks up from the designs to meet her eyes and Clara quickly diverts her gaze to the other council members.

"But I believe the water cost can be diminished by mixing in plant species that are able to draw water out of the air and efficiently collect and store rainwater or moisture from fog. Several species of cacti do this."

"Brilliant," Charles Daves says, drawing Clara's attention.

"Sorry," he says, flashing a smile. "I didn't mean to interrupt. Continue."

Clara's mind goes blank for a few moments and she takes a few seconds trying to find the words again.

"Regardless of fae lineage," Amor sends along their bond reminding her of a starting line from her practiced speech.

"Regardless of fae lineage, all fae have evolved alongside plant life and my designs include a wide variety of species to make sure every fae who enters can experience that connection to their evolutionary lineages," Clara says, thankful for the help.

"As a half-nymph fae, my personal connection to plants is very important to me, and having someplace here in Celeste where I can connect with a variety of plant life would mean the world to me, as I'm sure it would for many of the other nymphs who live here in Celeste. I ask that you consider my proposal," she finishes, bowing her head to the council.

Daves and several of the other council members nod back.

Elise Harthrone says "Thank you, Clara Glade. We will certainly take your proposal into consideration and let you know of our decision within the next ten to twenty days."

Clara bows her head again.

"Thank you," she says before returning to her seat.

"I think that went alright," she whispers to Stella and Amor as she sits between them.

"You did awesome!" Stella whispers, "Definitely the best presentation so far."

"Thanks," Clara whispers back.

Amor puts his arm around her pulling her closer to him, and all remaining tension in her body relaxes. They remain seated as the fae with the scroll continues to call the other presenters and they each share their proposals.

Once another four proposals are presented, and the last presenter has stepped off the floor, Elise Harthrone stands again.

"Thank you all for joining us for this session of the Beltane Council meetings. You have given us a lot to deliberate on.

"I hereby call this council meeting to a close. Feel welcome to stick around for tea and cookies."

The council members stand and exit through the door from which they had entered, while fae on either side of the floor stand and leave through the front. Clara and her family file along behind the fae until they have exited the main doors.

In the foyer, where they had entered hours ago, several tables have been set with trays of various cookies and mugs next to large jugs of steaming tea.

At the sight of the dark liquid, Clara feels drawn to the table. She quickly fills a cup before stepping out of the way of other fae perusing the cookie options.

"Clara, right?" a silky voice behind her speaks.

Clara spins around to see Charles Daves in front of her. Rather Charles Daves's tie, as that's what she sees first, before looking up to meet his sterling white smile. His height reminds her of the farming tower as he looms over her.

"Sir. Daves," she stammers, stepping back.

"Please, call me Charles. I am so happy you came in today and truly enjoy your passion. The council has yet to make its vote of course, but I'd say your proposal has a good chance of being approved." He winks one of his silver eyes.

"Thank you, Sir," Clara manages to say, awestruck.

"I was wondering if you would be interested in meeting with me to discuss some of your designs. I would love to offer my professional opinions," Charles offers.

"That would be amazing, Mr. Daves!" Clara blurts out.

"Please, Clara, Charles," he insists, placing a hand on his chest.

"I would really love to hear your feedback," she pauses before adding, "Charles."

It feels weird referring to a council member so casually, but Charles smiles broader as she says it.

"I shall have my assistant contact you to set up an appointment," he says, nodding his head regally before excusing himself.

Did that really just happen?

"You alright?" Amor asks, coming up beside her with a towering stack of five different cookies in his hand. Blushing, Clara realizes he can probably hear the excited screaming in her head.

She laughs and nods.

"Charles Daves offered to give me feedback on my designs," she says excitedly. "And said he thinks the council will approve my proposal."

"That's fantastic!" Amor replies. "Want a cookie?" he adds, offering her the pile.

Clara laughs taking the one on the top.

"Thank you," she says, kissing his cheek before running off to tell Stella and her moms the good news.

Pride grows in her chest as she thinks of all that has brought her here. She could have let fear keep her from sharing her designs with the council or talking things through with Amor, but she didn't, and because she didn't, she had Amor and she had hope that everything else was about to go her way.

# Need more?

195

If you're craving more of the story, go to http://moonlightcoven-publishing.com/passionflower-petals-deleted-scenes/ for extra content.

If you find yourself unwilling to wait to find out what happens next, request early access to the next book in the series, "Passion-flower Tendrils", at http://moonlightcovenpublishing.com/shop/passionflower-tendrils-early-access/

# Author Note

This book began as a dream that sparked an idea for a love story. I quickly learned that it takes more than a spark to keep the fires of creativity burning long enough to write a book worth publishing.

There were many times when the fire would dwindle to embers and frustration would set in. I began to use songs, books, and TV shows as kindling to keep the flame lit but the thing that worked best was sharing my work with my family and friends. Their feedback and praise would keep my hearth glowing for days and light a fire under my ass.

I offer you this story as kindling for your own creative endeavor and would be happy to be a friend if you need someone to share it with.

Lastly, if you've made it this far, and you enjoyed my book (or even if you didn't), please consider leaving a review on my website (Moonlightcovenpublishing.com) or Amazon/Kindle. I greatly appreciate your feedback, and your reviews could help other readers decide whether or not they want to read my book.

Thank you so much for reading!
-Jasmine Stark